For Crying Out Loud

C. P. Whitaker

Writer's Showcase
presented by *Writer's Digest*
San Jose New York Lincoln Shanghai

For Crying Out Loud

Writer's Showcase
presented by *Writer's Digest*
an imprint of iUniverse.com, Inc.

For information address:
iUniverse.com, Inc.
620 North 48th Street, Suite 201
Lincoln, NE 68504-3467
www.iuniverse.com

ISBN: 0-595-09950-5

Printed in the United States of America

For Paula
Whose belief, support and above all,
patience made this work possible.
Unconditional love is a wonderful thing.

Prejudices are what fools use for reason.

Voltaire

Prologue

Monday June 7, 1999 1:00 PM   Jackson, Mississippi

Marissa realized there would be precious little left of her BMW by the time she reached Alex. She just prayed it would hold together and that she wasn't too late.

There'd never been any doubt in her mind where Alex had run to. Lost Rabbit had been a favorite brooding place for years. A secluded, little known spot on the northwest side of the reservoir, it had been the setting for many a tall tale as well. Ancient catfish as big as Volkswagens. Three day long, sleepless, drunken camping trips. Fishing off of French air mattresses while towing a cooler of beer in a tiny blowup raft dubbed "Scooba Junior". Marie, the wonder Doberman, and her magical Frisbee. A group of friends helping bury Alex's first Husky, Kezia, on a cold and rainy December evening.

Yes, this is where Alex would go. 'Dear God don't let me be too late', Marissa prayed out loud, her voice cracking and nearly hysterical. The bile rose in her throat and she forced it back. She pushed the little car even harder over the washboard, backwoods road.

*   *   *

She'd been at Eric's motel room to tell him it was over when Alex roared into the parking lot in their old Jeep Wrangler. Staring out the room's picture window, Marissa had braced herself for the coming showdown. But there was none. Alex hadn't even glanced in their direction but had simply leaned in the passenger window of her car, returned to the Jeep and sped away. Then it all became a blur. Eric trying to change her mind. Taunting her. Telling her Alex was no good for her. Derisively asking her what kind of 'daddy' did she think Alex could possibly be? Demanding that she stay with him for the sake of their unborn child. Grabbing her. Trying to kiss her. Hands all over her. She had finally shoved him backward over a chair and bolted for the door.

Pulling out of the lot she headed for home. Home and Alex. Where she now knew without a shadow of a doubt she wanted to spend the rest of her life. Hoping and praying that she would find understanding and forgiveness for what she'd done. How confused she had been, yet again. She had tried to form a coherent and understandable explanation as she sped down city streets oblivious to red lights and stop signs. Twenty minutes later she was pulling in their driveway.

There was a dip where the gutter ran in front of the drive and the bounce always jolted her glovebox open. She'd been after Alex to fix one or the other for almost a year now. Automatically reaching to slam the little door shut, her heart caught in her throat. Except for an owner's manual and a city map, it was empty. The gun Alex insisted on her carrying for her protection was gone. Marissa scrambled for the garage door opener. As the door rolled slowly upwards she had seen what she feared most. Alex hadn't come home.

*   *   *

Tears began to well in her eyes and she almost missed the hidden turn that would take her down into Lost Rabbit. Alex had a good thirty to forty-five minute head start on her and had the advantage of being in the Jeep. The path (it didn't really qualify as a road) ended in a clearing that faced the wide-open waters of the Ross Barnett Reservoir. The Jeep was parked to one side near the water and the stereo speakers had been set on the hood. The ritual was a carryover from Alex's undergraduate days at Millsaps. It consisted of a pack of cigarettes, a six pack of beer, and Meatloaf's Bat Out of Hell album at full blast. The object was to have decided how to deal with the issue at hand by the end of the last song.

When the little car came to the backwash ditch, Marissa was forced to go the rest of the way on foot. As she got out of the car she strained to hear what song was playing. The wind blowing off the water was strong and brought the words to her effortlessly.

The final verses of the final song. And how appropriate that the one about bearing his child was playing at that very monment. Marissa looked down at her bulging belly and back towards the edge of the water. She couldn't see Alex but a puff of blue cigarette smoke wafted over the bank. She screamed Alex's name and the wind caught her words and carried them back to her as the music continued its soulful march onward.

Marissa struggled through the silt and the muck of the backwash. The gooey Yazoo clay sucked the flat from her right foot but she didn't waste time retrieving it. Once on the other side, she cradled her belly in her arms and began to run as fast as she was able. She hardly noticed as briars and rocks tore at her bare foot. All her energy, all her thoughts, her entire future was wrapped up in this singular effort. She had to reach Alex. She had to tell Alex. She had to stop Alex before…

She paused to listen. The last stanza…oh god…dear god, please don't…

Marissa reached the Jeep drawing ragged breaths. She knew she didn't have the strength or the time to go any further. Everything seemed to move in slow motion. Blood pounded in her ears. Dizziness overtook her. The baby kicked. Eric's baby. Oh, Mary Mother of God, what have I done?, she asked herself.

She looked down to where the tiny embryonic foot had connected with the wall of her uterus, then across to the rock-lined bank, and back to the CD player. As she watched the LED readout slowly ticking her future away, it dawned on her. Turn the music off. Surely Alex will come investigate.

Marissa leaned into the Jeep, stretching for the knob. Her fingers brushed it once, twice, before she was able to grasp it. It began to turn.

The knob clicked in the off position. The music died. And so did a vital part of Marissa when she heard the lyrics 'when you're crying out loud' mix hauntingly with the sharp report of a gunshot.

*   *   *

Monday June 7, 1999 9:00 PM   6th floor St. Dominic's Hospital

"I did *not* try to kill myself! Will someone please listen to me? And for God's sake, Sharon, get me a scrub suit. I refuse to wear this ridiculous gown."

"Alex, now lie back and try to relax. You just got out of surgery and you need to rest."

"I will hardly be able to rest with my ass flapping in the wind for all my co-workers to see. This whole thing is embarrassing enough as it is. Why, with Jackson having five hospitals, did they have to bring me to this one?"

"*They* didn't bring you anywhere. Marissa did. As I understand it, she half dragged half carried you to the car. Not a mean feat in her condition. And of course she's going to bring you here. It's the closest and you'd lost a lot of blood. Be glad she didn't stop to take your petty idiosyncrasies into account or you might have died. And you know we have the best suicide intervention team around, you're the one who designed it, ironic as that may be."

"I'm telling you I did not try to kill myself! What is wrong with you people? Shooting oneself in the ass is about as effective, suicidally speaking, as jumping from the window of a parked car."

"Alex, I'm sorry. As I understand it, you wrote the book and the hospital's merely following it. The spousal report, also designed by you, taken upon your admittance indicates you were under extreme stress, experiencing difficulties in your relationship, had gone off into isolation, were despondent, most likely drunk, and intentionally took a .38

with you. You just shot way off the chart on your very own scale, no pun intended. And according to you *and* the great state of Mississippi, you will be spending a mandatory seventy-two hours under psychiatric observation. Like it or not. Need it or not. And, since the hospital's chief clinical social worker seems to have been recently shot in the ass, you should be glad that your second in command had the sense to ask Marissa if you had a preference for a therapist or you'd be forced to spill your guts to some gawking resident instead of me."

"Sharon, you've known me since I was in Grad school. Granted it's been a long time since you last patched up my psyche but you know I'm not the type. I slipped on the rocks and the gun went off. It's as simple and as stupid as that. I've got to know that you believe me. And by the way, unless you want to end up a statistic yourself, don't let Marissa hear you calling her a 'spouse'. She says it makes her feel like a small houseplant."

"I do believe you, Alex. But you're stuck. How would it look if you didn't have to follow the same rules as everyone else? I'll keep my notes in your chart to a bare minimum. And I'll do Marissa's outpatient therapy, too, if you like. That'll keep a lid on the specifics. However, there's no way you can keep everyone from knowing you just had a bullet removed from your butt and, in general, how it got there. Don't think I'm going to let you slide for three days either. After all these years you wouldn't have asked for me if you didn't want to talk."

"Okay, okay. I appreciate you taking care of Marissa. Other than that people can think whatever the hell they want to. As for talking there's only one person I want to talk to right now and that's Marissa. I know I only get ten minutes a day for the next three days. I wrote that part, too. After that, if you think you're up to it, I'll talk. But I'm warning you it'll be a marathon session."

"You've got a deal. I'll go get her. And I'll even see if I can rustle up a pair of scrubs."

✴   ✴   ✴

"Owwwwwwwww."

"Oh, Alex, be still a minute. Here, lift up. That's it. Okay, your ass is covered, so to speak. Do you feel less vulnerable now?"

"Very funny. How can you joke at a time like this?"

"Because if I allow myself to cry I'd never stop. Alex, I already felt as if I'd lost you emotionally. You went way down deep inside yourself and locked all the doors behind you months ago. I know that's how you deal with things and you usually come back, but it scared me. And then when I heard that gun go off, well, I thought I'd lost all of you, forever. And all because I thought I wanted an easier road to travel. I'd rather go down the rockiest path with you by my side than have smooth sailing with anyone else. I know that now."

"Gee, counselor, you must be upset. You're mixing your metaphors."

"Now who's being flippant?"

"Some things never change, do they? I love you Marissa. I realized 'out there' that I even loved you enough to let you go if that's what would make you happy, cliché as that may sound. I want to spend the rest of my life with you. And if you want that too you've got to go into it with eyes open. We're going to have a child to raise. Eric's child. Here in the Bible belt some people are going to think that's scandalous. So be absolutely sure it's what you want. Because I'll never let you go again. Not without a hell of a fight."

"Okay you two, time's up. Time to get moving. You can see each other again in the morning. Marissa I'll walk you out and show you how to get to my office and we'll set you up an appointment for tomorrow. And as for you, Alex, I'll be back shortly."

*   *   *

"Okay, tough one, I'm back and I've got cokes, ice, nabs and a semi-comfy chair. You do realize what a sacrifice this is working in this drab setting, don't you?"

"I suppose since we have a previously established therapeutic relationship you don't feel the need to be brimming over with warmth and acceptance thereby winning my unwavering trust and compliance, huh? So where do you want me to start?"

"How about the beginning?"

"The beginning as in how I got this hole in my butt or the beginning beginning?"

"They're ultimately the same. Aren't they?"

"Well then, it was this incredibly cold day in Chicago…"

"What?"

"You said I get to pick the beginning."

Alex

Part One

1

You're sure you want to hear this? Okay then, but get comfortable. It's one hell of a story. It all began on a bitterly cold day at the end of January 1996 in Chicago. I was coming in from the Teen Center after having gone to the grocer's to pick up dinner. You know, pasta, bread, cheese, wine, a good book, that kind of stuff. I'd had a day of yelling kids, gangbangers, runaways, HIV positives. The usual, unfortunately. And all I wanted to do was eat, drink and read it all out of my mind. I juggled the grocery bags into the elevator in my building and right before the doors close this woman that lived down the hall from me jammed her briefcase between them and wedges them back open. Like she can't wait for it to go five floors up and back again. Chicagoans are like that. Or maybe it's just Yankees in general. Always rushing around like their clothes are on fire. I never got used to that. And they never look you in the eye or pass the time of day with you either. Gave me the creeps. Anyway, this old decrepit elevator starts groaning its way to our floor and true to my nature, I tried to make small talk with this woman. I mean we're neighbors, you know. Now don't give me that look. You're jumping ahead. Yes, she also happened to be incredibly attractive but that's not the point.

The old elevator ground to a jaw jarring halt. Trying desperately not to sound like a hick from Mississippi, I turned to her, gave her my most winning smile and said, "I imagine the trip to hell as being infinitely more enjoyable than riding in this contraption." Witty, semi-sophisticated, friendly. Nothing doing. She gave me this disinterested half smile, half nod. Same as she'd been doling out for the past several months. So much for being neighborly. So I thought, 'Don't worry honey, we'll pick up who-ever this is and then ride up one more floor, where I will gallantly stand aside so you can make a mad, paranoid dash to safety behind your door with a zillion locks and spend the remainder of your evening leisurely inspecting your emotional armor for any damage'.

Except the door didn't open. "Shit!" she says and starts jabbing the door open button. When there's no response she began this rapid-fire attack on all the buttons including the one labeled door close. I thought, 'oh that's brilliant'.

"Shit, shit, shit! I hate this god damned piece of junk!" She practically hollered and her fit and furor escalated to an off balance door kicking session with one hand on the rail and the other one combing the hair out of her eyes after each shot. I mean, here's this dark, lovely creature in high heels, designer business suit, manicured nails and appropriately accessorized with an eel skin briefcase no less, having an all out hissy fit in an elevator. It was all I could do not to burst out laughing. The ice queen had some fire in her after all.

Just as I feared, she suddenly turned on me. "What are you looking at?" she snarled.

I expected her to foam at the mouth any moment. I leaned against the back wall and crossed my arms and my ankles, cocked an eyebrow and said, "I am woman hear me roar?"

"Very funny", she snapped. "Did you give any thought to helping?"

"As soon as I'm sure I won't be impaled on those pumps I'll be glad to." And with that I confidently pushed off from the wall, stepped up to the control panel, and pushed the alarm button at the uppermost cor-ner. The one button she had neglected in her crazed attempt at escape. It emitted a sound like a small farm animal passing gas. So much for coming to the rescue.

It was hard to tell if she was wiping away the perspiration that had beaded on her upper lip or if she was trying to conceal a smirk. Either way it was the most human gesture I'd seen her make. She didn't let the opportunity pass though, to get in a, "What now, genius?"

"I suggest we force the doors open to get an idea of where we're stuck. For all we know we could just step right out."

"Be my guest," she said.

Be my guest. She said it in that way that made me want to screw up my face and waggle my head back and forth and mock her like a sixth grader. Instead I settled for, "What? Afraid you'll break a nail?"

And she got me again! "No, I just assumed it would hurt your ego if I did it without you."

Well, that did it. I grabbed each side of those doors and strained with all my might. I prayed it would work because that elevator was getting way too small, way too fast. And to add insult to injury, I couldn't get them open without her help. At that point I figured that if we couldn't just climb up to or hop down to the nearest floor, perhaps there would be enough room for me to at least leap to my death. But noooo, when they finally popped open there was nothing but a dingy brick wall covered with graffiti staring back at us. I'd have sat down and cried but I didn't want to give the woman anymore ammunition.

So there we were. Trapped, which was bad. Together, which was worse. I decided to take a different tack. The knight in shining armor routine was getting holes shot in it to the point that it looked like a sieve. So I gave up trying to impress her and tried to figure out how to tolerate her. It didn't seem to have dawned on her exactly how long we might have to share those cramped quarters.

Even as tall as I am I wasn't about to play movie hero and go climbing through that trap door, shinnying up the cables to the next floor. And yelling was useless. There were only three tenants left in the entire building, me, her and little Ms. Applegate on the second floor who was deaf as a fence post anyway. As far as I was concerned we were reaping our just desserts for not gettin' while the gettin' was good. We'd had two months notice that the building was coming down to make way for some nauseating architectural monstrosity that was going to house God knows what. We had two weeks left and I had no idea where I was going. I hadn't even taken the time to start looking.

I could tell our lack of options was starting to sink in with her. She was pacing like a caged animal. And that's not easy in an elevator, let me tell you. It reminded me of those wind up toys that run into a wall and keep backing up and doing it over and over again. I managed to resist the urge to say 'ding' every time.

Every man for himself seemed the best approach so I just slid down into the corner, pulled out my book and started to read. That went over like a lead balloon.

"How can you be so calm? We are trapped in an elevator in case you haven't noticed!"

I don't know what got into me but I slammed my book shut and jumped up with this horrified look in my eyes and started pacing back and forth with her, wringing my hands and saying, "Oh my God. Oh my God! We're trapped in an elevator! What'll we do? What'll we do?"

"Idiot."

"Guilty as charged," I replied and sat back down and started to read again. "By the way, are you claustrophobic by any chance?"

"No. Why?"

"No particular reason. I just thought it would be the icing on the proverbial cake if you were."

"Well, regardless of that fact, I refuse to spend the night in this elevator. And I'm damn sure not going to do it with you!"

"Awwwww," I said, "and just when I thought you were starting to like me. What do you want me to do? Jump? Because I would if I could. Right now a five floor free fall is beginning to look pretty good."

"Look, I don't know you but I know about you, okay? I'm not stupid. I know all about your kind. If we're going to be stuck in here let's get one thing straight. You so much as touch me and I'll scream bloody murder."

I think she realized the futility of that statement as soon as she said it. So she scrunched herself into the opposite corner, wrapped her skirt tightly around her legs and put her briefcase in her lap.

You know me. I wasn't about to let that pass. So I played it to the hilt. I cocked my eyebrow like it really hadn't dawned on me till she mentioned it but now that I thought about it, it seemed like a prime opportunity. Now don't give me that look. She deserved every bit of it.

Her eyes got as big as saucers as I slowly peeled off my jacket, exaggerating every movement. I could see her eyes flick to my arms trying to decide if I was strong enough to do what she thought I was about to do. And I have to admit enjoying that deer-in-headlights look she got when she realized I probably was. I shook out my jacket and laid it out between us on the floor like a pallet. She hoisted that briefcase up in front of her like a shield.

I dropped my voice down to kind of husky and breathless and said, "Take off your shoes."

"Oh God, please don't hurt me. Please just leave me alone." I didn't know a grown woman could curl up into that small a ball. I was starting to have some guilty twinges and if she'd started to cry I would've felt like a real shit. But I had a point to make and I was going to make it.

"We can do this the easy way or we can do it the hard way. Now give me your shoes." I started to lean over towards her and she reached down with a shaky hand and slipped off her heels and handed them over. "Now, that's more like it."

I reached into my pocket and pulled out my tiny Swiss Army penknife and set it on my jacket beside the shoes. Then I reached behind me into my grocery bag and pulled out the two bottles of Merlot that I'd picked up on the way home.

Still uncertain as to where all this was going she managed to squeak out a, "What are you going to do to me?"

I looked her dead in the eyes as I reached back into the bag and said, "I'm going to do to you what any red blooded American Southerner would do given the opportunity. I'll even give you a hint. It's a four letter word and it starts with 'F'."

2

"I'm going to feed you." And with that I pulled the loaf of bread and the cheese out of the bag and laid them on the jacket. I tossed her shoes back to her and said, "So if you would kindly take those spiked heels of yours and push the corks in on those bottles I'll make us some hors d'oeuvres, such as they are. We have bread and cheese, cheese and bread, bread and bread, and last but not least, cheese and cheese. Which would you prefer?"

I was so busy basking in my coup and prattling on, I didn't notice that a storm was brewing over in the corner. I glanced up just in time to fend off a pump that was hurtling towards my head.

"You are the biggest asshole I have ever met!" she hollered at me.

I just grinned at her and said, "Actually, I don't think we've been formally introduced. My name's Alex. Alex McKinley."

I would've put out my hand but I was afraid I'd draw back a nub. So I left it at that, which seemed to suit her just fine. She harrumphed a couple of times and then engrossed herself in some work she pulled from her briefcase, which by the way, she placed between us as some kind of unspoken barrier. I was beginning to feel like Clark Gable in It Happened One Night. So I took her shoe, poked the corks in on both bottles, slid one in her direction and settled down to read and eat my meager dinner.

I had to give her credit. She held out for a good hour. It was getting to her though, I could tell. After awhile, every time I took a bite or a sip

I could hear her sigh. Even though I told myself I was ignoring her, I was acutely aware of every move, every sound she made. It must've been about eight o'clock when she finally put her paperwork away. And twenty minutes of nothing to do but drum her fingers was about all she could take, thank God, because it was about all I could take, too. She let out this big sigh like she was deflating and said, "My name's Marissa. Scafidi." She paused for a second then added, "And I'm sorry about all that earlier. I come on a little strong sometimes."

"That's okay," I told her, handing her the untouched bottle of wine. "I tend to be a little overly sensitive."

She rummaged in her purse, pulled out a deck of cards, held them up and waggled them back and forth. I took this as an invitation and nodded my head. I laid her briefcase on its side for a card table while she shuffled. She laid the stack down, I cut them and she picked them up to deal. She dealt five cards each, looked at her hand, laid three cards down, picked three up and then stared at me. I just stared back because I didn't know what the hell we were playing.

She got this incredulous look on her face, "Poker. You do know how to play poker, don't you?"

To which I shrugged and said, "No. Am I supposed to?"

She started collecting all the cards and plucked mine from my hand all the while muttering, "God, I don't believe this."

I felt myself getting indignant again. "What you don't seem to be able to believe is that your assumptions are false. You've assumed that I have some excessively high level of testosterone that presupposes what I do and don't know; what I am and am not capable of doing. From what I've observed, you've got more balls than I do. Figuratively speaking, of course."

I thought we were headed into round three but she just threw her head back and laughed this wonderfully deep, hearty laugh. She picked up her bottle of wine and raised it in a toast. "Touché", she said. Then she dealt five cards each, spread the rest of the deck on the briefcase and told me, "Go fish."

By some unspoken agreement neither one of us said anything except 'Go fish' to each other for the rest of the night. Why spoil a good thing? It just seemed safer that way. It's even turned into a code word for us. Anytime we get into a heated argument, when it gets to the point where we think we're about to strangle each other, one of us will pop out with 'oh, go fish' and we'll dissolve into giggles. It certainly sounds better than, 'oh, fuck off' and it breaks the tension.

So we played and drank and drank and played for several hours. It was kind of strange. For two people who did not want to be stuck together we didn't ever discuss how or when we thought we'd get unstuck. I don't remember feeling *too* terribly drunk but Marissa was getting pretty tipsy. She started out sitting up straight, then after awhile leaned back, then a little while later began listing to one side and then eventually ended up propped up on one elbow. It wasn't too long after that, while I had taken an inordinately long time to decide whether to ask for the aces or settle for threes, that I looked up from my hand to find her sound asleep. I covered her with my jacket and sat against the wall and watched her.

Sleep is so terribly deceptive. Even the most caustic take on an aura of serene harmlessness. I reminded myself not to let my guard down.

3

I woke to a bouncing, screeching sensation that didn't quite register to my muddled brain until I peered sleepily up at a grundgy beer-bellied construction worker whose pants were about to succumb to the weight of his tool belt. He gave one look at two disheveled occupants of the elevator, the empty wine bottles and the rest of the disarray and said, "You weirdoes will do it anywhere, won't you? Get the hell outta here before I call the cops."

We were so glad to be released from our cell that we didn't even try to explain. We just scooped up our individual belongings and stumbled out into the lobby. Marissa looked at me sheepishly, glanced at her watch and said something about being late for work if she didn't hurry. We both looked at the elevator, then at the stairwell, then back at each other. I grabbed the door and held it open for her and she headed for our floor taking the steps two at a time in her stocking feet. I could have easily out distanced her but I lagged behind, unable to stop myself from shamelessly enjoying the view.

Both of us reached our floor winded but at least we got there this time albeit twelve hours later than originally planned. We went to our respective doors, put our keys in the locks and turned them. I thought I would be stealing one last unnoticed glance at my former cellmate before we returned to our separate lives, but I was surprised to see that she had paused to do the same. I smiled and wiggled my fingers at her.

She pretended to be picking some nonexistent something or other off her doorjamb, coughed and went inside.

'Well fine,' I thought, 'if that's the way she wants it then I have more important things to concern myself with than whether or not the uptight, pump throwing witch down the hall likes me. Even if she does look angelic when she's asleep. And sexy as hell when she's throwing a temper tantrum'.

I forced myself to focus on the more important things. Like getting to work on time and finding a new place to live. And getting one of my favorite and most promising bad ass troublemakers out of the juvenile detention center before they decided to try him as an adult habitual offender and lock him up for good.

I quickly went through the ablutions of getting ready and took one last look in the mirror to see if I looked as bad as I felt. I did.

I headed out the door and lo and behold who almost knocks me down? She was moving so fast I didn't even get to watch her descend the stairs. I was all prepared to do mental recreations of one of my favorite Picassos starring Ms. Scafidi. But instead I was relegated to listening to the staccato clacks of her heels echo in the stairwell. Oh well, it was sweet while it lasted.

4

I checked in at work. Inquired as to the crisis du jour. Grabbed the community coat, shirt and tie that I forced all my juvy defendants to wear for their hearings. I made a mental note that it was getting threadbare. No surprise as many times as it had been put on and taken off lately. I headed to youth court.

I met Van Go in the holding room and gave him the clothes. He grimaced but put it all on. He knew better than to put up a fuss since he knew he could go down hard this time.

Actually his name was Carlos Giuseppe Diaz. His mother was African American; biological father was Hispanic and long gone from his life. Everyone at the Center started calling him Van Gogh after he spray painted a great self portrait on one of the bathroom walls. He was really quite an extraordinary talent. When a group of boys at the Center formed a basketball team to play in the city league, sponsored by yours truly since the board of directors wouldn't spring for it, I told the kids I'd pay the entry fees but couldn't afford shirts. So they all got white T-shirts and spray painted their names and numbers on them. Carlos' shirt was a work of art except he spelled his nickname V-A-N-G-O, so he was Van Go from that point on.

It was almost time. I took out a comb and ran it through his hair, yanked the earring out of his ear and stuck it in my pocket. We were escorted to a table in a large room set up like a court room you see on TV except spectators weren't allowed and there was no jury box. It was just a room for hearings but there was still a judge and usually an attorney of some sorts representing whoever was opposing letting the kid go. In this case it was going to be one of the attorneys for the City of Chicago of which there's umpteen zillion.

Now you know me, and you know I've always been very eclectic in my beliefs. I've never been able to follow just one set of rules. Have always been able to see two sides to everything. Personally, I think it's one of the reasons I'm so good at what I do. So, I could look at what happened next in one of two ways. Either Marissa Scafidi was a boil on the butt of humanity sent from hell to make my life miserable and haunt me wherever I went *or* fate was throwing us together because we had some deep learning to impart to one another. Zen as I try to be, I was leaning toward the former because who of all the gazillion lawyers in the city was sitting at the table across from us but *her*. Remember the music they played in Psycho during the shower scene? That's what I heard in my head when I looked over at that table.

But I don't think I was nearly as stricken as she was. The look on her face when she glanced up from her papers as we walked in was priceless. You would have thought I was the ghost of elevators past come to spirit her away to some ghastly netherworld.

She jumped to her feet. "Your honor I object."

"What in the world do you object to, Ms. Scafidi? The fact that the defendant showed up? Sit down."

"I, uh, I'm sorry your honor. No, it's just…uh nevermind. My apologies." She shot ocular daggers in my direction and I flashed her my winningest smile.

We went through the typical blah, blah, blah of a juvenile hearing and Marissa was acting like it's the trial of the century and she's Marcia Clark.

"Your honor, Mr. Diaz is a known repeat offender who has been in and out of the system since he was ten years old. He is now sixteen years old and the City wishes that his minority status be revoked and that he be treated as an adult in this latest charge."

In a stage whisper I said, "You can revoke all you want but he'll always be a minority and therefore treated with less leniency than a white upper class kid from the suburbs."

"That's not what I meant and you know it," she shot back.

We were both on our feet at this point. "But that's what's really at the bottom of all this. He's just a kid without the benefit of a well-heeled, two-parent family. He was expressing his angst."

Throwing her legal pad on the table and putting hands on hips she said, "Well he got his angst all over the side of City Hall this time."

"Looks a damn sight better now if you ask me."

"Well, nobody asked you. And who are *you*? His fairy god mother?"

Rap, rap, rap.

"Actually I prefer guardian angel. But be careful, I might wave my magic wand and make you disappear."

Bang, bang, bang. "Excuse me!!"

"In your dreams," she hissed at me.

"Silence!!" For a split second I thought it was the great and powerful Oz but it was only the judge.

Before I could stop I heard myself saying, "Pay no attention to the man behind the curtain."

The judge boomed, "I beg your pardon!"

Marissa looked absolutely appalled, began to turn beet red, let loose with a bleat of laughter and slapped both hands over her mouth in sheer mortification.

I sat down. She sat down. Carlos said, "Aw man, I'm goin' to jail for sure."

As it turned out Carlos was in a lot less trouble than we were. He was remanded into the custody of his mother and given forty five days to paint over his 'mural' at City Hall with flat white paint. A fate worse than death in his eyes. The judge called us into his chambers. Actually, I think he just liked being able to say that out loud in court because he didn't have anything but a hole-in-the-wall office. What he *did* have was the power and authority to call it anything his self important little heart desired. I felt like I was being taken out behind the woodshed and told to pick out my own switch.

I was banned from showing my face in any of the youth courts for six months. I argued that my kids would suffer but the judge vehemently disagreed with that. I gasped. Marissa smirked.

Marissa was ordered to provide forty hours of community service. She argued that her grueling schedule seeking justice for the law-abiding citizens of Chicago would not permit it. The judge said at the Teen Center. Marissa gasped. I smirked. Then I gasped. The judge smirked. Justice was done.

5

I didn't see hide nor hair of her for a week. Not at the Center and not at the brownstone either. I figured she'd managed to weasel her way out of the judge's orders. I couldn't decide how I felt about it but didn't have much time to dwell on it. It took all my spare time trying to find another place to live before they tore my building down around me.

After looking at thirty-two places that I wouldn't let my dog live in, if I'd had one, I found a decent duplex in a quiet neighborhood that was still semi-thriving on the outskirts of town. It would be a bit of a commute but I could afford it and there didn't seem to be cockroaches big enough to carry me off in my sleep, which is more than I could say for the other places I'd seen. And the biggest plus was that the other side was empty and I was mulling over leasing it, too. Possibly for a private practice office. I'd been hemming and hawing over the decision to quit the Center and strike out on my own seeing private clients. I was getting too old to worry about being shot every day. I figured in private practice I wouldn't have to worry about it but once every month or so. So I took this as an omen that it might be time to try it.

I talked three of my biggest and most trustworthy kids from the Center into helping me move that next Saturday. Well, bribed is more like it. After much negotiating it came down to twenty bucks apiece and all the pizza they could stuff down. They thought it was such a good deal that they each showed up at the apartment with a buddy who 'needed the money real bad, man'. All of who were wearing tennis shoes and Starter jackets that would have taken two weeks of my salary. It was just as well, though, because the elevator was on the blink again and we had to carry everything down five flights of stairs. When it was all said and done I was out a hundred twenty bucks cash, fifty bucks worth of pizza, a Sony Walkman and a sports watch. Both of which I noticed days later had mysteriously disappeared. That, plus the cost of the rental truck wasn't too bad all things considered. Not to mention we made the entire move in just under three hours, but then all my worldly belongings didn't even fill a fourteen foot truck and two thirds of that was books.

We had just finished unloading at the new place. I was hovering around trying to take a mental inventory of everything and decide where to put it while Van Go was navigating the myriad of wires for the stereo. Tyrone was on the phone ordering the pizza when my new landlord walked in. He was a squat, balding, constantly perspiring little white man who seemed unnerved to find himself surrounded by my multi-ethnic contingent of moving assistants.

"Ah, friends of yours, ah…I'm terrible with names. Can't ever remember them. McKinley isn't it?" he quavered.

"Yessir," I said, "but please just call me Alex." The boys had gathered in closer, curious to see if I would acknowledge them as friends or relegate them to something more like wards under my constant supervision. I did a little of both to appease both sides. "Yes, these young men are friends of mine. They participate in the activities at the Center."

"Oh, I see. Fine then. That's fine. So, is everything okay? Getting settled and all that?" he asked.

"Yes, it's going nicely, thanks. And I'm glad you're here. I came to a decision last night about the other side." I started herding him through the door so we could talk outside.

I'd spent a sleepless night the night before weighing the advantages and disadvantages of going private. As long as I stuck to the purely logical, analytical aspects then all things pointed to it being the right move. I had some savings and if I tightened my belt I could survive while building a solid client base. Therapy was where my strong points lay naturally and academically. I'd make much more money. Set my own hours. Not answer to a board of ivory tower, out of touch bureaucrats. And I could get up in the morning, get ready for work and walk through the connecting door into my office. What more could one want? But then I had paced across the room and was face to face with the picture montage the kids at the Center had given me. Granted, I had taken all the pictures of the kids and our activities. And had them developed. And kept them in a locked cabinet at the Center which they had to jimmy open in order to get to them. And they put the collage in a frame they took off a large print I had hanging in my office. But it was still one of my most cherished possessions.

So, I decided to do both. Stay at the Center, rent the office space, see clients at night. I don't abandon the kids and I don't let go of the dream. I get to work myself to damn death, save the world, not let anyone down, and fix everyone else so I don't have time to look too closely at myself. Sounded good to me.

"Well, ah Alex, right? I'm glad you mentioned that," he stuttered as we walked across the lawn. "That's one of the reasons I'm here. Wanted to let you know you're going to have a new neighbor. Didn't hear from you all week. Figured you'd decided against it. Couldn't let it just sit there." He was inching his way to his car the whole time and I stayed in step with him while he stammered on, "No sir, had to turn it around. Gotta pay bills you know. Nice lady. You'll like her. Ah, give her this key when she gets here. Rent's due on the first. Need anything give me a call. Gotta run."

He half-heartedly clapped me on the back as some sort of apology and got in his car and sped off. I just stood there staring down at the bright, shiny gold door key in the palm of my right hand.

I felt dizzy so I backed into the shade of the rental truck and sat down on the passenger side running board. While I was trying to decide whether I was going to *ex*plode or *im*plode, a white panel van pulled up to the curb. A word at the top in a semi circle had an 's at the end, some-body's name I guessed, but all I could make out from where I was sitting was 'Plumbing and Repair' and what looked like a telephone number underneath. Two dark haired guys in their early twenties got out. They leaned against the side of the van and one pulled out a cigarette and lit it. God, what I would've given for one of those. I'd given up smoking years before but still wanted one on a daily basis.

"This it?"

"Yeah, looks like it."

"I thought she said there was a white movin' in next door. All I see is a bunch of niggers and spics sittin' on the porch. That's not gonna cut it."

"And all I see is a couple of wops leaning on a truck," I snapped, glad to have an outlet for my building inner rage. I didn't feel like beating myself up for letting my dream slip through my fingers. That would come later, I knew. Right then I wanted to vent. I got up from my seat and started walking towards them.

"Who the fuck'r you? And who you callin' wops," the older looking one said.

"I'm the whitey that's moving in next door. And I'm calling you a wop. Don't dish it if you can't take it."

"We didn't call you nothin'. Hell, we didn't even see you sittin' there. Them niggers and spics must be workin' for you."

"Those African American and Hispanic young men happen to be friends of mine who are helping me move."

"Oh great," he says poking his buddy on the bicep with his elbow, "Sis is movin' in next to a fuckin' politically correct, left wing, bleedin' ass heart liberal."

I could feel myself 'bowing up' as my Grandaddy used to call it. "Look you redundant sonofabitch. First of all it isn't any of your damn business who or what I am or am not. Secondly, who do you think you are to stand here slinging racial slurs about people you don't even know while you get pissed off when I refer derogatorily to your ethnicity? You double standard assholes owe me an apology." Self-righteous and pontificating. I was feeling better already.

The big one took a step towards me but the other one reached out and put an arm across his chest and shook his head saying, "Hey, it's okay. We don't want trouble. We're sorry. Okay? It's cool."

That really surprised me. I was thinking I must be tougher than I thought I was. "Oh, well, uh good then. That's more like it. I don't want any trouble either. Like Rodney King said. Right?"

They looked at each other and back at me and said, "Who?"

"Nevermind. Here, give this key to your sister. It goes to her side. Landlord left it." And I turned around to go inside. All the guys were standing behind me listening to the exchange. I regretted using the profanity but was glad to have modeled expressing myself without resorting to physical violence. It would be a good lesson for them.

"Come on guys, show's over. Pizza's here. Let's go inside and eat."

6

"You a fool, Mac. They coulda squashed you like a bug." Tyrone told me this while washing his pizza down with one of my beers.

"Hey! Where'd you get that? I bought Cokes for ya'll." I looked around and realized they all had a beer.

"Pizza ain't no good without a cold one," Antoine piped in. "'Sides Ty's right, they'd a wanted you they'd a had you."

"I don't care," I said. "I had right on my side."

Tyrone laughed. "I don't care you got right, left, north, south, east and west on yo' side. Even if none of 'em is any bigger than you, you still gonna get squashed. You don't know what you doin'."

"I keep trying to tell you guys that it's not size or fire power. I won didn't I?"

"No, but you still alive and that's somethin'" Van Go grinned.

I'm getting indignant by this point and say in a pouty voice, "I did too win. They apologized didn't they?"

Lavon stood up, all six feet five inches of him. "They apologized because you had six big bad ass niggers and spics standing behind you ready to tho'down if they'd laid one finger on you." They burst out laughing and passed high fives all around at that.

Trying to save face, I corrected myself and said, "Oh. Well then, *we* won."

Tyrone grinned from ear to ear. "Yeah, I keep tryin' to tell you Mac. Size and fire power, man. Size and fire power."

We all sat there for a while eating pizza, drinking beer and truly enjoying each other's company. Me trying to figure out one, how I was going to explain why I was letting them drink beer in my home if the Center's Board of Directors ever got wind of it, and they would, they always did; and two, how I had come to have such a unique relationship with these kids. They respected me as an authority figure, albeit a good natured and caring one, at the Center. And they treated me like a friend, one of the 'homeys', away from work. Me, an adult, over-educated, overly analytical, sometimes pompous, Southern honky from the heart of racist Mississippi. Go figure. Whenever I would ask them why, they always had the same reply, 'because you're real, Mac'. I was never really sure what that meant exactly. Maybe because most of my life I'd felt anything *but* real. Somehow they seemed to see through that, though.

As I glanced around the room, I noticed the guys were quieter than I'd ever seen them. There was a Bulls game on, but that usually fired them up so it wasn't that they were reverently watching Michael Jordan do his thing. They seemed almost contemplative. Not a word I often used with that bunch. Maybe they were wondering why I was letting them drink my beer, too.

It didn't last long. All of a sudden, Van Go lets loose with a loud, "I'll be fucked! Will you look at this shit!?"

I thought for a moment maybe Rodman had gone off half-cocked and beaten up an innocent spectator but instead Van Go headed for the front window and was motioning for the others.

"I ain't believin' this shit, man. You see that? That's the attorney bitch that got Mac in so much trouble with that judge."

"Carlos!!"

"Yeah Mac?"

"Get rid of the 'B' word!"

"Oh yeah, sorry. It's the attorney witch. What the fuck she doin' here?"

I pushed my way through the mass of bodies at the window to take a look.

"Gentlemen, it appears she's moving in."

7

Now down here in the good ole South you know that we would have all just piled out of the house and helped my new neighbor move in. But up there's a different story. Besides that, the guys were too busy discussing which they should do first, slash the tires on her BMW or rip off her electric meter. I convinced them to do neither and even extracted a solemn promise from them that they'd never seek revenge for what happened in court that day. I reminded them that as far as we knew she still had to do community service at the Center and that I didn't need my next door neighbor any angrier or more resentful with me than she already probably was.

Full of pent up energy and having no immediate outlet for it they decided to head home. To show them how much I did trust them I let them return the moving truck for me. As they left I told them to 'Be Nice' and as I shut the door I heard them giving Marissa and her brothers what they call their imitation of 'proper white men'.

"Good evening gentlemen."

"Oh, my, what a charming sofa you have there."

"Lovely evening for a stroll, isn't it miss?"

I looked out the window in time to see three of them climb in the back of the truck, three get in the cab and as they were pulling out of the driveway Tyrone, who was sitting in back, waggled his fingers at Marissa and yelled, "Ta ta!"

I knew somehow that performance was going to cost me but it was worth it. I can't remember when I've ever laughed so hard. And the confused look on the faces of Marissa and her brothers was priceless.

Until that day I would have argued against the possibility that a person could experience two completely opposing emotions at exactly the same time. But as that afternoon came to a close I sat in my big overstuffed chair, peeping out the blinds at the goings-on next door and was simultaneously thrilled and mortified. I recognized the mortified part immediately. It took awhile for me to accept that deep down I was also inwardly delighted. I mean, she was the absolute, single most infuriating woman I had ever run across and I'd only been in her physical presence twice. This would probably turn out to be my worst nightmare. It was certainly bad enough enduring her cold, unneighborliness when she was down the hall but now, now I'd be sharing a wall with her! Which got me thinking, 'oh great, she's beautiful, moderately successful and single. I'll probably be spending a lot of time listening to her headboard banging against the wall, too'. Yes, that was rude and uncalled for but I'm just trying to tell the story as honestly as possible and I *did* think it.

As much as she seemed to dislike me, I figured I could go introduce myself as her new neighbor and in the time it took to say community service she'd call the landlord, break the lease and pack her stuff right on out of there. Not a bad idea. And it would have solved my office space problem to boot.

So I knew something was up when I not only didn't do that but made a special effort not to be seen by her for at least a week. I was up and out at the crack of dawn telling myself it was as good a time as any to go to the gym before work. And I came home under the cloak of darkness telling myself that I had lots of unfinished work and filing that I needed to stay late and take care of. I knew that what I was doing was making sure I wouldn't run into her. That was no big surprise. But when I finally realized *why* I was doing it, that made me stop in my tracks. I didn't want her to see me until she was good and settled in so she'd be less likely to up and leave.

8

Since the early mornings and late nights were about to kill me, I decided to just get the showdown over with. I went inside and prepared my props and then went to her front door and knocked. When she opened the door I held out an empty cup and said. "Hi neighbor, could I borrow a cup of sugar?"

She stared at me like she was brain dead for few seconds and then said, "What the…where did *you* come from?"

"Next door, hence my use of the term neighbor," I replied.

"Next door? Next door as in down the street or next door next door?"

"That's right. Next door next door as you so eloquently put it. So, how 'bout that sugar?"

"I don't have any sugar!"

"Oh. Well then, you'll be needing this." And I brought my other hand out from behind my back, which was holding a cup full of sugar. I even gave her my very best Cheshire Cat grin to go with it.

She rolled her eyes and leaned her head against the door. "Please, just go away."

"Okay, suit yourself. But you haven't seen the last of me."

As she shut the door in my face I was sure I heard her mumble, "That's precisely what I'm afraid of."

I considered knocking again, thought better of it and went back to my side. Round one was over and in my estimation it was a draw.

I put on some music, classical I think, so if she could hear it she wouldn't think I was a complete boor. I lay on the couch listening to her stomp and bang around on the other side and wondered why I cared.

I spent two long years on your therapist's couch working through my issues of people pleasing, my fears of not being liked and accepted. I made it through all that with flying colors. I'd reached a point where if someone didn't like me it was their problem, not mine. Unless, of course, I like them. I still get hung up on that one every time.

So, the only unfathomable conclusion I could come to was that I liked this woman. She hadn't exactly shown me anything likable. But there was a connection there, nonetheless. It was there in the elevator whether we wanted to admit it or not. It hovered like a live electrical wire, too hot to actually touch but sparking ever so often just to let us know it was still there.

At this point all I was thinking is friendship, believe it or not. No really, for several reasons but even if it went further you've got to start out as friends, don't you? I knew anything else right off the bat was out of the question and I wasn't even sure I wanted that. I'd been burned pretty badly my last time out and had decided to give up women for lent, maybe longer, and that was three years before Marissa. You go that long and you almost forget about it. Besides, she didn't fit my pattern. I've always tended to fall for women who needed rescuing either from themselves or someone else and Marissa could no doubt take care of herself.

I didn't really have any adult friends in Chicago. I suppose my expectations were entirely too high. The only people I knew were my Board of Directors and I didn't see any sense in spending time with people who had the personality of wet cardboard. Life's too short and I'd just as soon read a good book. I've always wanted my friends to challenge me and push me to my limits. And I'd always needed my lovers to swoon in genuine adoration and devotion in order to keep my insecurities and fear of abandonment at bay. Therefore, since

Marissa had obviously never swooned over anything in her life but *was* most definitely a challenge to say the least, friends it would have to be. If I could only figure out how to get her to cooperate.

9

I decided the approach should be subtle, persistent, not too invasive and above all charming. There was an inside connecting door in my hall which I knew from having toured both sides of the house, led into her hall. There were two deadbolts in the door. One that could only be locked from my side and one that could only be locked from hers. There was about a half-inch gap between the bottom of the door and the hardwood floor.

I waited a few days after the sugar fiasco and then began sliding notes under the door. I started simply enough: 'Have a nice day', 'Happy Friday', 'How's the weather over there?' All to no avail. Well, I say to no avail but she hadn't boarded up the gap and she hadn't charged me with stalking, so that was something. I progressed to sliding a few jokes under and actually heard her laugh out loud once.

The big breakthrough came one night when I heard the distinct sounds of the Wizard of Oz coming through the walls. I turned on the TV and ran through all the cable channels and it wasn't on any of them, so she must have rented it. Then I remembered her not only getting my Oz wisecrack in the courtroom but she laughed out loud. Like a hyena. And to cinch it all, I could hear her rewinding the tape to listen to Garland sing Over the Rainbow several times. 'This is it!' I thought. I had found a common denominator in the equation!

So I slipped a note under the door asking her which of the characters she thought she was most like. It was the first time I got a response back.

When I saw the folded piece of paper on my hall floor I thought, 'BINGO!' I opened it up and read: 'I must be Dorothy since this is all beginning to seem like a bad dream!'

I didn't care. She'd written back and that was something. I'd had enough clinical training to know that a negative response was better than no response. And she seemed to like to communicate in back-biting sarcasm.

So I wrote back: 'And I must be the Scarecrow since only someone without a brain would keep trying to be friends with someone who is obviously incapable of being civil'.

I got a note back saying: 'Toto, I have a feeling we're not in Kansas anymore. I think we've gone to duplex hell!'

And I responded with: 'I'll get you and you're little dog, too!'.

To which she replied: 'In case you haven't noticed, I don't have a dog. Now, stop this nonsense'. And she flipped off her hall light. I thought, 'This is great! It's like primitive E-mail'. I decided not to push my luck so I honored her request and didn't write back. But the best part of all was that I noticed her hall light go on and off every fifteen minutes or so for the better part of an hour and a half. She was looking for the next note! I finally went to bed with a very self-satisfied grin on my face.

I spent the majority of the next morning calling every toy store in the city looking for a stuffed Scottie dog. Of course the only one was halfway across town. I picked it up on my lunch hour, went by a pet shop and got it a collar and a tag with TOTO engraved on it. I left work early so I could beat her home and leave it on her doorstep.

I must have paced a hole in my rug waiting to hear her car drive up. I realized I was being ridiculous, bordering on pathetic, but I couldn't help myself. Things were painfully silent next door for almost an hour. It was close to nine o'clock when I saw a slip of paper slide halfway under the door. Yes, I admit it. I'd been sitting there waiting for it. When I picked it up it was blank. My heart sank. Then I heard a soft voice on the other side say, "Thank you." It was all I could do to muster up a "You're welcome." She was quiet for a moment and I thought she might be gone but then she said, "Goodnight Alex." I said "Goodnight Marissa", turned off the hall light and drifted toward my room in a half daze.

As I lay there reviewing the day it occurred to me that I might be on the road to being smitten. But I quickly dismissed that as a silly notion seeing as I hardly knew the woman.

10

Things got a little crazy at work and kept me away from home a lot over the next few days. Or maybe I just made things crazy because I was feeling crazy. I kept asking myself what I was doing. What was I thinking? Why was I drawn to this woman? I didn't know her. But an inexplicable part of me felt like I did. I don't believe in coincidences. Everything happens for a reason. Why over the past month did we keep getting thrown together? Was there something I was supposed to learn from the situation or, more specifically, from her? My motto has always been, every moment is a teachable moment. Everyone has something to impart to you if you'll only allow yourself to be open to it. So what was this? There was only one way to find out.

I went home and printed an invitation on my computer:

> You are cordially invited
> If you have no other plans
> To join me for an evening in OZ
> 8:00 PM Friday March 1, 1996
> On the other side of the door
> Dress is casual
> Refreshments will be served
> PS
> Evening includes:
> 50th Anniversary Edition Video
> 39″ TV Screen

Stereo Surround Sound

Garland Never Sounded So Good

I slid it under the door that Wednesday night. I figured at best I'd have company and at worst I'd watch my favorite movie and get drunk.

Friday night rolled around. I'd straightened up the apartment, popped popcorn, set out a bucket of iced down Rolling Rock beer, and put a bottle of Merlot and a glass on the coffee table not knowing her preference. There was soda and iced tea in the fridge but I was looking to loosen her up some, so she'd have to ask for those. *If* she showed up.

I couldn't believe how nervous I was. This was by no means a seduction scenario. I just wanted to get to know her. But I was still as nervous as a long tailed cat in a room full of rocking chairs.

She'd been very quiet over there since she'd gotten home so I had no way of knowing what her plans were. For all I knew, on a Friday night, she might have a date. But she'd spent every night at home for the last three weeks so I decided the odds were against it.

At about ten till eight o'clock I made a loud production of unlocking the deadbolt on my side of the connecting door. Nothing. At five till I checked myself in the mirror one last time. I looked fine, very casual in jeans, sweatshirt from my favorite outfitters and tennis shoes.

At eight o'clock I popped in the movie, got all the gadgets set just right, opened a beer and got settled on the couch. Disappointed but determined to enjoy myself. At about five minutes after, Garland was starting to sing. As a last ditch effort I turned the volume way up. Other than books I didn't own anything of much value. But I love my movies and my music almost as much as my books and I had put together quite a system.

I had my eyes closed as every word reverberated through the house. About halfway through the song I could feel her presence in the room.

When the song was over I opened my eyes and could see her in the light from the TV screen, leaning against the archway between the living room and dining room with her hands behind her back and Toto at her feet. I reached for the remote and paused the video. She looked very tentative standing there and I didn't want to make any sudden moves and scare her off.

"Would you like to see it from the beginning?" I asked.

She nodded. I started rewinding.

"The lights are off so they won't reflect on the screen but you can turn them on if you like."

She shook her head. I started the video over and turned down the volume some since she was actually in the room now. I made no comment about her standing between rooms assuming she'd sit down in her own good time. I also made a concerted effort to watch the screen and not her in case she was watching me and not the screen.

About the time Dorothy's house plopped down in the Merry Ol' Land of OZ, Marissa came and sat down on the far end of the couch, but not before gingerly placing Toto between us.

I smiled and said, "Guard dog?"

She smiled and said, "No. Just thought he should learn about his roots."

I placed the bowl of popcorn on the couch between us and offered her a beer which she accepted. I placed the bucket on the floor between us, effectively creating a popcorn/dog/bucket barrier which seemed to put her at ease. We watched the entire movie in silence except for the appropriate chuckles, gasps, sniffles etcetera.

When it was over and we were sitting in the light of a blank TV screen I reached for another beer and realized we had drunk them all. Which then made me painfully aware of the fact that I needed a bathroom break. I excused myself and knew this would be the big test. Would she still be there when I returned? On my way back I stopped at the fridge and got another two beers, more out of hopefulness than self-confidence. When I got to the living room the lamp beside the couch was on but she wasn't there. I noticed movement across the room and saw her squatting by the bookshelves reading the titles.

"So," I said handing her a beer, "Do we have similar tastes?"

"As a matter of fact we do," she replied. "In fiction at least. Your non-fiction's a little out of my realm of thinking."

"I fancy myself an eclectic thinker so there's no telling what you'll find there."

"I see that."

I sat on the couch and watched her. She seemed much more at ease. She had on a black turtleneck with an oversized University of Chicago hooded sweatshirt over it, black sweatpants and old driving moccasins, no socks. Dressed like that she didn't look quite so intimidating.

She stood up and said she needed to excuse herself. I asked if it would be temporarily or permanently. She hesitated so I picked up Toto and said I was holding him hostage. She just shrugged her shoulders and left the room. A few minutes later she came back, kicked her shoes off and sat cross-legged on the couch facing me. She motioned for me to hand over Toto. She put him in her lap and fiddled with his collar and tag. She took a sip of her beer then looked me dead in the eyes and said, "So. Why do you want to be friends?"

"You're a very good attorney, aren't you?"

"Yes I am. Now answer my question, please."

"Yes ma'am," I said and saluted her. "Do you want the cut and dried version or the flowery and flattering version?"

"You don't know me well enough to flatter me."

"Okay then. Here goes. I don't know why. Or at least the reasons aren't the typical ones. My outward experience of you has been that you are uptight, caustic, sarcastic, closed-minded, straight-laced, opinionated and when push comes to shove just down right bitchy."

"I am not closed-minded," she said rather indignantly.

"Well we can argue that another day. My inward experience of you is that you are intelligent, responsible, trustworthy but not trusting, have a wonderful sense of humor, are very sensitive, and probably cry when you watch Little House on the Prairie. You love animals so much so that you don't have one because you couldn't spend enough time with it and

I suspect you prefer cats. You have a deep seated value system that you hold to so firmly that it keeps you from realizing your ambitions; you're a dreamer and a romantic and you've been hurt deeply by someone you loved—hence the suit of emotional armor. Oddly enough, I like all those contradicting traits in a friend. Keeps things from getting boring. How am I doing so far?"

"Who *are* you?"

"I am an alien being sent to study your kind. I can see through walls and read minds. But do not be alarmed. I mean you no harm." I barely got the last few words out before Toto bonked me in the forehead.

She snatched him back on the rebound. "I'm serious. How do you know all that?"

"I don't know how, actually. It's not something I've thought about consciously until you asked and then it all just spilled out. I'm sorry if it upsets you. I just feel like I know you."

"I don't know if I want you to know me." She curled up a little tighter on the couch.

I took a chance. "Yes you do or you wouldn't be here. As closed off and protective as you are, you wouldn't have put up with my antics for so long and you wouldn't have walked through that door tonight if you didn't. You sense *it* too, whatever *it* is, don't you? Don't you?"

She started fidgeting. "All right! Yes! And it's freaking me out, thank you very much." She stood and slowly paced the floor like it was a closing argument. "As best as I can tell, you are the exact kind of person that irritates the hell out of me. And I can't seem to get away from you. And what's worse is I think I'm starting to like you in spite of yourself!"

I smiled up at her. "Thank you, Counselor. That's all I was looking for. Confirmation that I'm not the only one going crazy here."

"Believe me, you can't feel any crazier than I do right now. And at the risk of seeming rude, while the first half of the evening was enjoyable and the second half was, ah, interesting, I hope you understand if I say I need to sleep on this."

I stood up. "Nope, doesn't seem rude at all. It seems honest. I expect that from a friend. Always say exactly what you need, want and expect."

"You *are* from another planet, aren't you?"

"No, just getting too old and too tired to play games."

She nodded, picked up Toto and headed for the door with him tucked under one arm. We stood there, she on her side, me on mine and had an awkward moment. I leaned on my side of the door facing and she started to close the door. She dropped her head, cut her eyes up at me, smiled bashfully with one side of her mouth and said, "Goodnight, Alex."

I grinned back as she was closing the door and said, "Goodnight Marissa." Right before the door completely closed I added, "Oh, and Counselor, if this is going to be a friendship, I'd like it to be an equal one. The next move is yours."

11

She must have had to sleep on it a lot. I didn't hear a sound on the other side all that weekend except for assorted kitchen noises and the occasional toilet flush. No TV, no music and no contact. Her car didn't move from its spot, not even on Sunday and I knew from the past month that she was a regular church-goer. Was I being hyper-vigilant? Yes! I admit it. It was driving me nuts. I don't know what possessed me to leave it all up to her. But I managed to control myself and not push it.

We saw each other as we left for work Monday morning. She was cordial enough but gave no clue as to what was going on in her head. I was cranky as all get out that day and by the time I got home I had decided to hell with it. Who needed her? I didn't care. Fine.

I was able to maintain that attitude until Tuesday night. There was a slip of paper waiting for me in the hall. On it was the word 'dinner' with a question mark. I flipped it over and the other side was blank. I thought, what the hell is that supposed to mean, 'dinner?'. Dinner when? Where? Dinner in? Dinner out? She cooks? I cook?

So I wrote back, 'yes', and slid it under the door. It went back and forth like this all night: 'Friday?'. 'Yes'. '7:00?'. 'Yes'. 'My place'. 'OK'. 'I'll cook'. 'Sounds great'. 'Spinach manicotti?'. 'Sure'.

I couldn't decide if she was being playful, scatterbrained or nervous. It didn't really matter. I was glad she was going to give it a chance.

It seemed like I just sailed through the rest of the week. Next thing I knew it was Friday. I left work early, picked up a bottle of wine, contemplated flowers but didn't want to overdo it. When I got home around five o'clock Marissa was already there. She must have cut out early, too. That was a good sign. When I walked in my side I was hit by the most wonderful aroma. Wow, sarcastic, belligerent and she could cook, too!

You would have thought I had a date that night, as nervous as I was. I got a beer to calm myself down and headed for the shower. She hadn't said what to wear and I stood staring into my closet for so long that I needed another beer. After that one was gone I seemed to be feeling *much* better and the decision making process started to flow. Not too slouchy, not too dressy, I opted for khakis, a pullover olive green sweater and leather boat shoes.

When that was all said and done I still had another thirty minutes to kill so I got a beer and sat down to channel surf. By the time seven o'clock rolled around I realized I was feeling really great, not nervous at all, until it slowly dawned on me that it was because I had a really good buzz going. I was showing up for my first dinner invitation tipsy! I didn't have time to do anything about it, so I took several deep breaths, put on my most sober face, grabbed the bottle of wine and knocked on the door.

In response I got a lilting, sing song, "It's open." Lilting? Sing song? I must have the wrong door. Or maybe it's a trap! I snickered at that and stuck my head around the door to scout it out. The coast was clear and the smells coming from the kitchen would have been too much to resist anyway. I pretended I was Toucan Sam and followed my nose. 'Oh, God', I thought, 'she's going to know I'm drunk. I'm thinking drunk thoughts!'

The kitchen was a whirlwind of activity. Either that or my vision was blurry. There were pots and pans everywhere, some dirty, some clean, dishtowels strewn all over the place, different food items in different stages of preparedness on the stove, the countertop and on the small table in the corner by the window. Marissa was flitting from one workstation to the next, completely at ease amidst the chaos. She glanced up long enough for me to offer the bottle of wine. "Oh good," she said as she kept working, "I thought I might have to send you out for more. I'm afraid I started without you."

It was then that I noticed an already open bottle on the table with half the contents gone. She had needed a little fortifying herself to get through the evening. I was wondering what to do with myself when she asked me if I would put on some music, motioning with a large knife towards what I assumed was the living room.

Her apartment was arranged identically to mine except it was a mirror image. Off the kitchen was a dining room in which sat a beautifully set table. I was pleased to see that she had gone to quite a bit of trouble. There were navy blue linen placemats, white dinner plates, navy blue charger plates with gold moons and stars on them, with white salad plates set inside them. There was a gold runner down the middle of the table with crystal candlesticks and white candles; wine goblets with cloth napkins poking out of them.

Most of her furniture looked either antique, Bombay Company or possibly Ethan Allen. Actually, very much what I would have had *if* I'd had any money. It was all a collection of different styles and periods that blended well together. The difference was in the accessories. Where I tended to lean towards dark and brooding, she leaned more towards light, airy and feminine.

The living room was more of the same. It all suited her very well. She had several paintings on the walls and it was interesting that they all had a fantastical or little girlish, fairy tale quality to them. I don't mean to say they were childish or immature works. They were actually very detailed and very good, just not what I would have expected.

I found what passed as the stereo and made a note that I would have to teach her something about quality electronics. She had a rack of CD's and as I started going through them it occurred to me that the choice of music would set the tone and send a message for the evening. I read through the titles several times. She had a lot of classical, some

Broadway and movie soundtracks, and a lot of easy listening/lite rock male vocalists with a heavy dose of Michael Bolton. The pressure of choosing was getting to me. I decided on the soundtrack to CATS.

I had seen the show when it came to Chicago. As a matter of fact I had taken some of the kids from the Center to see it. It was a mix of upbeat and mellow and if she had seen the production it would give us something to talk about if the conversation lagged.

When I got back to the kitchen she handed me a glass of wine, said that everything was almost ready and motioned me towards the little ice cream parlor type table. I sat and watched. I'm a watcher in case you haven't noticed. I mentally record every detail I can.

She had on black slacks, a white silk blouse with one too many buttons unbuttoned for my current state of inebriety, and black dress loafers. I noticed a black and white checked blazer hanging over the other chair to complete the outfit. It was too hot in the kitchen for it even for the second Friday in March. She had an apron on that said, 'The first bottle's for the cook'. I asked her if she took that literally. She smiled a tipsy, crooked smile and said with over exaggerated hand motions, "I'm Italian. I have no idea how to cook stone cold sober. In your honor I am limiting myself to half a bottle head start."

"I hate to disappoint you but I had three beers before I got here to calm myself down. So I'd say we're about neck and neck."

"Oh? Nervous are we?"

"I'll admit to it if you will," I said.

"You really go for this equality stuff, don't you? Or is that just what you think women these days want to hear?" She handed me the bottle I brought and a corkscrew and said, "Here, make yourself useful. If we don't open it now we might not be able to manage it later."

This was going much better than I had expected. I found myself thinking that one of these days we would have to try and be around each other without alcohol but I wasn't sure we were ready for that just yet.

"Okay," she said, "Everything's ready." She started tugging at the apron string behind her neck. She was petite enough that had she not tied it up it wouldn't have served much of a purpose. She had it tied to where the loop was too small to slip over her head. She fumbled with it for a second, sighed and said, "Give me a hand, would you?"

I got up and went to help. She had her hair up very loosely in a bun and little tendrils had fallen down across the back of her neck. I wasn't thinking about anything more than releasing her from her self induced bondage until I got close enough to start working on the knot. I was trying so hard not to touch anything but the knot, very conscious of not doing anything that could possibly be misinterpreted. But then she reached up and pulled those wisps of hair out of the way and I felt my knees momentarily get weak. Everybody has their preferences, eyes, legs, smiles, breasts, and I'm not saying I'm without those. But my biggest weaknesses are a little more complicated. Surprise surprise. I have weaknesses for images, scenarios, and that was one of them. I could smell her perfume. I would have asked her what it was and slept with it on my pillow, but I thought that might be too obvious.

"Oh, by the way," she said as she swayed ever so slightly, "I've decided I might be able to like you."

"I'm honored." I tried to keep my breathing slow and even.

"Well, you should be."

I bit my tongue, literally and figuratively, and concentrated on the knot. Just as I got it undone, she was starting to lean back against me.

I made a big show of, "Hey! There we go! Okay! What can I take to the table?"

She pulled off the apron, collected her thoughts and began to direct traffic. When we finally sat down across from each other the look on her face told me that she knew she had momentarily given in to something she didn't quite understand

12

Dinner was incredible. Marissa had baked bread from scratch. We had salad, asparagus, and spinach manicotti. I was in heaven and told her so several times. She seemed very pleased with herself, as she should have been. Conversation flowed smoothly as did the wine. Nothing of any grave importance was said. It was mostly chitchat but the company and the comfort level were delightful.

When we were done, she started clearing the table and told me I could go sit in the living room and she'd join me in a minute. I took the dishes out of her hands and told her that the least I could do in return for such a meal was wash the dishes and that she could go relax. She asked me if I was always going to be the opposite of what she expected and I told her, most likely, yes. We compromised by doing it together. I washed; she dried and put away. When we were done she poured us two after dinner liqueurs in small brandy snifters. I followed her to the couch.

Marissa's side of the house was the one that had the original fireplace and the remodelers had kept it, adding glass doors and some other more modern appointments. We were both just drunk enough to dispense with formalities, so without asking I went about building a fire. She went to the stereo and put on a CD called Stormy Night, which was classical music combined with the sounds of a thunderstorm. When the fire was going good I got up and began a closer inspection of the paintings on the walls. Marissa curled up on the end of the couch and I could feel her eyes follow me around the room.

"These are wonderful," I said, "Where'd you find them? They all seem to be by the same artist but none of them are signed. Is he or she local?"

"What makes you think they're by the same artist?" she asked, her tone dripping with doubt.

"I don't know anything technical about art. I only pay attention to the feelings it evokes in me. And all these, while very different in a lot of respects, *feel* like they came from the same soul."

"Okay, I'll play along. You're telling me you can feel the soul of that artist just by looking at those paintings? Sounds like new age bullshit to me."

"No, no, no. I'm not talking about airy, fairy granola bar stuff. I'm not going to burn incense, chant and then suddenly name the artist. What I'm saying is that art, good art, comes from the soul, not the mind. So, to me, when an artist creates a work, they're trying to say something that they can't say in words because it comes from deep within them. I think it was Emma Goldman that said 'Art is part of a rebellion against the realities of its unfilled desire.'"

"Where do you get all this stuff?"

"I don't know. I'm blessed, or cursed depending on how you look at it, with one of those minds that retains everything."

"That's a frightening thought. So, go ahead, tell me about this artist's soul." She had an 'I dare you' look on her face.

"I don't know if I can do this half-drunk."

"I don't think you can do it at all. But you started this, you don't get to back out now."

"That sounds like a challenge," I said raising my glass to her. "And I accept the gauntlet that has been thrown down before me."

"Oh God, get on with it."

"Okay, here goes". I walked up to the large one over the mantel and asked her if I could touch it. She nodded, looking very skeptical. I took several deep breaths, unfocused my eyes and ran my fingers over the dried oils. I could feel the fire on my legs and hear the sounds of the storm coming from the speakers. "All the central figures are feminine in nature even though they are all fairy tale type characters—fairies, pixies, goddesses, damsels—so the artist is most likely female. Also, if the artist were male they'd probably be considerably more buxom so that says female artist, too. The foreground is always fairly light and airy, full of movement and positive feeling colors. The artist therefore yearns for freedom, freedom from themselves or society. There is a sense of playfulness, carefreeness and unself-conscious self-expression in the characters but it feels like this is an unfilled desire in the artist rather than a reality in her life. The background is dark and foreboding to a great extent in some of the paintings particularly this one, only implied or hinted at in the others. I mean, look at this one, with the fairy swinging in the tree swing but looking back over her shoulder at an impending storm. That tells me that she feels she has to sneak moments like these or that she feels it's not safe to behave like this at all, even though she wants to. That's the overt analysis. Now on to the pure feeling and energy of the work," I paused for a moment then closed my eyes leaving my hand on the painting. "The artist is scared and feels emotionally trapped. She had her childhood taken away from her and she resents it. She's bought into the image or role that's been created for her or pushed on her, that's why she can't even paint real people playing like children. Instead of feeling whimsical or day dreamy when she paints, she's closer to anger. She keeps all this stuffed way down inside and if she's aware of it at all she's certainly never told anyone. She can't even own these feelings enough to sign her name to her work where anyone can see it. She's..."

"Stop it!" Marissa cut me off in midsentence.

"Oh my God," I turned around to see tears streaming down her face. "She's you."

13

I walked over to the couch and knelt down on the floor in front of her. She had curled up into a semi-fetal position and was staring past me into the fire. She looked like a scared little girl.

"Tell me about it," I said.

"I think it's time for you to go home, Alex."

"I'm not leaving you like this. Talk to me."

"There's nothing to tell. You've caught me in a weak, drunken moment. That's all."

I turned around and stretched out on the floor with my head leaning back against the couch and stared at the fire. I don't know how much time went by. It was marked only with the occasional sniffle and sigh. After one particularly heavy sigh she got up, went to the kitchen, came back with the bottle of liqueur and poured herself a glassful. Before it was all said and done she would drain that one and another.

"I always had the sense that my father was disappointed that I was a girl. And my mother, because of that, seemed guilty and ashamed that she hadn't given him a son. Especially since for eight years it seemed like I was going to be the only child. Not because of a lack of trying, mind you. I lay in my bed night after goddamned night listening to him go at her. Not that I understood exactly what was going on but it didn't sound pleasant. The nights that I'd hear her tell him no, he'd hit her. After several miscarriages she got pregnant again and the doctor sent her to bed right before my eighth birthday. My birthday came and went without anybody noticing. I was so worried about her. I thought she was going to die. I ended up having to take care of the house and Pop and Mama.

Tony was born a couple of days before Christmas and Mama was really sick. Everybody was at the hospital but I was too little to go so I got farmed out to my aunt and uncle. We had Christmas after they brought Tony home and it seemed like everything under the tree was for him. Mama was never really the same after that. She was always sick or not feeling well. I ended up practically raising Tony myself. Pop was thrilled to have a son, so everything at home got a little better. Mama got pregnant again and went through the same trouble. Nick was born when I was ten and like the good daughter I just added him to my list of duties.

I would get up in time to fix breakfast for Pop, feed and bathe the boys, get Mama comfortable and literally run to school to get there on time. When I got home I'd fix dinner, clean house, wash clothes, iron my school and Pop's work uniforms, put the boys to bed and then try to do my homework. Mama helped as much as she could but it seemed to take so much out of her.

She slowly got her strength back and was able to take care of things herself around the time Tony was five and Nick was three. She never came out and said so but I could tell she resented the bond I had with them. She tried to establish herself as Mama to them but they kept coming to me when they wanted something. That summer when I was thirteen I got sent to stay with my aunt and uncle who lived out in the country and didn't have any children. It was supposed to be a reward for all I had done. I got 'rewarded' every summer till I went to college. End of story."

Anything I could have said at that point would have sounded trite so I just sat there with her. The fire had died down to embers and I was going to put another log on when I noticed soft, gentle snores coming from behind me. I took the empty glass from her hand, roused her enough to get her on her feet and guided her down the hall to what I guessed was her bedroom. It could have been the bedroom of an eight year old little girl with the all white wicker bed, pink and yellow and lavender accents, an antique porcelain tea set on one of the dressers and Toto nestled on the bed amongst a pile of pillows. In all honesty I was probably already falling in love with her by then but that moment was the first time it ever just welled up from inside me and engulfed me.

I navigated her to the edge of the bed and helped her sit down. She started unbuttoning her blouse while I pulled back the covers. She dropped her blouse on the floor, kicked off her shoes and tried to stand up with no success. She giggled and mumbled "help me". I helped her stand up and before I knew it her slacks fell to the floor. She stumbled as she tried to step out of them and I caught her and helped her under the covers before she shed any more layers. I tucked her in and smoothed the hair from her face. She looked up at me with unfocused eyes, reached up and grabbed a handful of my sweater and pulled me to her. "Alex," she slurred, "tell me something. Is it possible to hate someone and like them at the same time?"

"Yes, I believe it is," I said, assuming she was talking about one or all of her family.

"Good," she said as she reached up and patted my cheek, "'cause mostly I like you." And with that she rolled over, pulled Toto to her chest and fell asleep.

14

"Wake up, sleeping beauty." I was sitting on the edge of her bed blowing the smell of fresh coffee towards her across the top of the steaming mug in my hand.

"Mmmrrrpphhh rruugglle", she said as she swatted at me half-heartedly.

"Oh no, no, no. It's after noon. I think I've been more than generous." She stirred and wallowed for a minute.

"Goway." She tried pushing me off the bed from beneath the covers with her feet.

At some point during the night she must have peeled off that last layer of clothing because her bare shoulders were peeking out of the top of the sheet. Sure enough, there on the floor lay bra and panties, a cute little lacy matched set. I spotted a grey T-shirt hanging over the chair across the room, got it and laid it across her. I set the coffee on the bed-side table, said, "Breakfast is ready when you are," and went whistling down the hall.

A few minutes later a disheveled Marissa sheepishly poked her head through the connecting door. "Alex?"

"Yes, dear?"

I heard her mumble, "Uh oh," as she tentatively stepped through.

"Come in, come in. Don't be bashful. Your eggs are getting cold."

She gingerly came into the room and slid into a chair. "Uh, Alex?"

"Mmmmhmmm?"

"Uh, why did you fix me breakfast?" Her head was hanging and she was cutting her eyes up at me suspiciously.

"After last night? Are you kidding?"

"Alex...about last night..."

"Oh, yes, I'm sorry, I'm being insensitive aren't I? Please don't be self-conscious. I know you probably wouldn't have done it if you hadn't been drunk. And I probably did take advantage of that fact. But you did seem willing enough. Don't worry, I don't think any differently about you. Well, that's not entirely true. Actually, I feel closer to you. I hope that doesn't embarrass you. I mean no big deal really. That's what two people do when they like each other. Right?"

She slowly lowered her head to the table and gently banged her forehead on it while mumbling, "Oh god, oh god, oh god..."

"Marissa," I said as I reached over and patted her shoulder. "It's nothing to be ashamed of. It's a perfectly natural thing. Or at least it should be, in my opinion. I don't know why people are so uptight about it. It's always been my belief that if everyone made a point of doing it at least once a day the whole world would be better off. I mean, yes, it would take practice and some getting used to. You'd have to start off with someone you really felt close to and trusted but sooner or later you'd be able to branch out to friends, acquaintances, co-workers. Who knows? Eventually you might be comfortable doing it with the stranger on the bus seat next to you."

She kept rolling her head back and forth on the table and groaning every time I made a point.

"No really, this is exciting. Think of the universality it would create. The barriers that would dissolve. People would feel less alone and isolated. To keep it going you'd have to break racial and ethnic barriers, socio-economic barriers. The possibilities are endless."

I shoveled some more eggs in my mouth, swallowed and kept going, "Of course, it's all theoretical. But it makes sense. We should try an experiment. See if we can keep it going. If you don't have any plans this afternoon we could try it again. Don't worry, I'll take the lead this time."

Marissa's head popped up, "I took…oh god…the lead…last night?!" She started to stand up, shaking her head back and forth. "I can't handle this Alex. I'm sorry. I was drunk. I didn't know what I was doing."

"Marissa, hey calm down. It's OK. I had a not so great childhood myself. That's my whole point. You're not alone. And it's OK to talk about it."

"Huh?" She dropped back into her chair.

"You don't remember one bit of last night, do you?"

"Well, I…uh…some, yes…but ah…obviously not the part that seems to have been, well…so momentous for you."

"Well, isn't that interesting. Do you only do this when you drink or do you have selective amnesia anytime you allow yourself to be open and vulnerable with another person?"

"Now wait just a minute! I don't know what happened last night but whatever it was, it doesn't give you the right to start making assumptions about me. I resent that!"

"Resent it or resemble it?" I was enjoying myself.

"Look," she said as she stood up and threw her napkin down on the table. "I feel like shit and I don't want to deal with this right now."

I reached out and put a hand on her arm. "Marissa, please. I'm sorry. This is not how I had pictured this morning going. We had a very touching moment last night. I thought we had broken down a barrier. I thought we would move forwards, not backwards."

"Touching moment?! I just bet we did. For all I know the 'touching' as you call it lasted all night. How could you Alex? You've got to know I didn't want that. Or is that what turns you on? Is that how you work? Being cute and charming? Proposing friendship? Getting women emotionally vulnerable and then so falling down drunk that they put up no resistance? And you thought we'd have a nice little breakfast this morning and move *forward*?! I don't think so. Now let go of me."

Instead, I tightened my grip on her wrist and growled, "Sit down."

It must have been the combination of my tone of voice and the look on my face or the fact that I was squeezing her wrist much harder than I should have been. In any case, she sat.

"This would almost be amusing if you weren't so upset. And if I didn't have an idea of what's really going on with you, I'd be highly insulted. You tell me the last thing you remember clearly and I will fill in the blanks."

She remembered dinner, cleaning up, going to the living room, the fire and my beginning to scrutinize the paintings. From that point forward, nothing other than a sense of vulnerability and feeling violated until waking up naked with me sitting on her bed. No wonder she was freaking out. I went back and recounted everything she'd blocked out, in obviously disconcerting detail. She wasn't any more comfortable hearing it the second time around although she seemed relieved that nothing more had happened.

"How do I know for sure…"

I cut her off. "Marissa, you *know*. You're body knows. It knows that didn't happen. Listen to it. Your head's just trying to grab any reason it can to throw up a wall and run away. So just stop it. It won't work."

"So nothing…"

"Nothing."

"Thank God. I mean, I really thought…oh thank God."

"Okay already. You've made it quite clear what your worst fear was. Believe me, it does my ego a world of good to know how repellent the thought is to you. Let's just start the day over. I've got something to show you *if* we can ever get past breakfast."

I nuked our plates and coffee in the microwave and we ate in silence. All things considered, she seemed comfortable enough.

15

I knew if we went much longer in silence or if I didn't show her what I'd been working on all morning soon, that she would lose the relieved feeling of our not having slept together and begin to dwell on the fact that she had shared more about herself last night than she had intended to. So I scooped up the breakfast dishes, left them dirty in the sink and ushered her, hung over and complaining that it was cold, into the backyard.

I'd been up since the crack of dawn, inspired and ready to work. I had snuck back into her apartment to get the details right, sketched out some rough plans and measurements and gone to the neighborhood hardware store by eight o'clock. By ten o'clock I had a finished product all the way down to having stained it the exact color.

As we walked out the backdoor on my side I suddenly realized how presumptuous I might have been. I told her to close her eyes and she flat out refused. So I talked her into at least walking backwards. When we got to the huge old oak tree that had been mercifully spared the fate of its more modern subdivision cousins; I told her she could turn around.

For a moment she just stared, then she ran her hand slowly down one of the thick, camel colored braided ropes. She put her hand tentatively on the seat and gave it a gentle push. She watched it swing back and forth a few times then turned and ran back into the house slamming the backdoor which, unfortunately, automatically locked. In rapid succession I heard two other muffled door slams which I assumed were the hall door and her bedroom door.

I sat down on the swing, elbows on knees, head in hands and rocked for awhile trying to figure out what she had been so overwhelmed by. As time passed I managed to rule out joy, the cold, and my amazing craftsmanship.

You know, in my recounting all this I realize some of it sounds so calculated but it really wasn't. I was just being me. I guess a lot of it is due to my understanding people so well along with my feeling that I had some kind of unexplained understanding of Marissa on an even deeper level. I knew by this time that I was falling in love with her. I wasn't all the way there yet but I was well on my way and it was quite clear that it would never and could never be mutual. I knew that if we continued with our budding friendship, that one day I would experience the pain of watching her fall in love with someone else. And I knew I'd never tell her the full extent of my feelings. What I'm getting at, I suppose, is that none of my behavior was an attempt to 'win her over'. I accepted the circumstances as they were. I just wanted to experience the joy of being around her. Maybe I needed the gift of learning that I could feel deeply for someone without translating it into a full-blown intimate relationship. Particularly since I hadn't been very good at sustaining one for very long up to that point. And I felt I had gifts that I could give her in return. So far they'd gone unappreciated but, hey, I'm nothing if not persistent.

Anyway, I'm sitting in the swing starting to freeze my ass off and not getting any insights. I tried my backdoor on the off chance it hadn't locked but it had. I tried knocking on her backdoor. Nothing. I knew if it was anything like the previous weekend, when she had pulled a similar disappearing act, that I'd probably not get a response. I was beginning to think I had discovered a new affliction. Emotional narcolepsy. It could go hand in hand with the selective amnesia. Anytime you experience any intense emotions your defense mechanisms just flip a switch, you sleep like a rock for twelve to twenty-four hours and when you wake up, viola!, you don't remember a thing.

I went for a long walk to try and warm up, came back about an hour later, knocked again to no avail and ended up jimmying a side window and crawling in. It was late afternoon by that time and I decided to see if there was anything to my new theory and went to bed.

I hadn't forgotten a thing when I woke up the next morning. It was Sunday and I didn't want to hang out all day catastrophizing about what I might have done wrong this time, so I went to the Center. I liked it there on Sundays with no one else around. I thought I'd get some paperwork done but I spent most of the day in the gym perfecting my freethrows instead. Lost in my head and no better off by the time I left that afternoon. I had the top off the Jeep and took the long way home. The day had turned out unexpectedly pleasant for mid-March. Chilly but not unbearable. I pulled in the driveway in a little better mood. It was getting to be that dusky time of day where all you get are the last few slanting rays of sunshine before the sun drops over the horizon. I decided to go in, grab a beer and sit outside before we went back to having normal frigid weather in the next day or so.

With my hand on the back doorknob, I happened to glance out the window. There she was, highlighted by one of the last sunbeams of the day, swinging with all her might. I watched for a minute, then left her to her private childhood.

16

I didn't hear anything from her the rest of that night. I know now that Marissa likes to, and needs to, process every new experience and emotion until she's sure what she thinks and feels about it. It will always be frustrating but back then it was maddening. I never had any idea how long the process would take.

So you can imagine my surprise when she met me in the driveway when I got home from work the next evening. All smiles and excited, she practically dragged me to the back of the house.

"Hurry up, Alex. Come on before it gets too dark!"

I was having some difficulty adjusting to this complete turnaround but I trotted along behind without questioning it. When I caught up she was already in the swing and going higher than she had the night before. She kept saying, "Watch. Are you watching?"

"Yes, I'm watching." I wanted to add 'and how could I not? I can't take my eyes off you whenever you're within sight', but I controlled myself.

And then she jumped. Leapt. Soared. I'd never seen anything like it. Probably because you don't see many adults doing it in the first place. But even so, she had an airborne ballerina quality about her.

"I would score that a definite 10", I said, holding up imaginary cards.

She bowed and then clapped her hands in front of her face like a little kid. "I'm glad you think so. I've been practicing since I got home. I left work early and went by the park to watch the kids swinging. I realized last night I didn't know if I was doing it exactly right.

And then all of a sudden this little boy went sailing into the air and I knew I had to try it."

"Of course, you know what happens next don't you? Or didn't you stick around that long?"

Her expression started to fall. 'God', I thought, 'she's so fragile underneath that suit of armor'. I jumped in and headed it off before it continued. "To the Jeep. To the Jeep. Quickly now. Come along." I was marching towards the front of the house with my finger pointed skyward.

"Alex!? What are you doing?"

"Hurry up. No time to talk. We must follow through with universally mandated playground rules and etiquette. Get in the Jeep."

As we pulled into the road she was still asking where we were going. "Why, to get ice cream of course! Every perfect leap and dismount requires it. We have no choice."

"Ice cream? I haven't even had…"

"Not another word, young lady. I won't hear it. I simply won't."

We giggled and acted silly the rest of the way there and back. We went in the house on our separate sides but there was an immediate click and knock on the hall door. I opened it and she waggled a deck of cards at me and asked if I was ready to learn how to play poker. We played on my coffee table with an old movie on the TV for background noise. The little talking we did was nothing more than idle chitchat. We had nothing to bet so we played a point a hand. When she had thoroughly trounced me 100 to 16 we called it a night.

I walked her to the hall door, we said our most comfortable good night to date and I closed the door. Neither one of us locked our side.

17

The whole week went like that. We checked in with each other when we got home. Marissa used the swing as a way to transition from work life to home life. I stuck to my usual tradition of having a beer. By the end of the week we'd eaten together twice, watched a movie, talked daily, played cards, shared magazine articles, and just sat in the same room and read our respective books in silence. Even though things were going so well, I was getting nervous that Friday was quickly approaching. It seemed for some reason to be our bad luck day. I finally mentioned it late Thursday night. She felt the same way and suggested we skip Friday altogether. It was worth a try. We agreed on brunch, my side, Saturday at ten o'clock.

I knew I couldn't be at the house all night and honor our agreement so I badgered a member of my Board to pull some strings and get some last minute tickets to the Bulls game. For the sake of the kids, of course. He came through with five, which people in high places in Chicago, like him, can do at the last minute.

We worked on a point reward system at the Center so I took the three with the highest number of points for the week and made a plea to the rest to let Carlos have the fourth ticket.

Van Go never was quite able to make the point system work for him. But he was everyone's favorite and the closest thing to a son I'd ever had. He'd been moping around all week and acting out more than usual. Everyone seemed to know that it was a reaction to having only one week left to do his community service work. It was going to kill him to paint over his 'mural' on City Hall. It was the best work I'd ever seen him do.

I knew the City and the court were trying to make a point, but it would have cost them thousands of dollars to have one done professionally and it wouldn't have been half as good. His crowning glory was not only the work itself but that he did it in broad daylight over the course of two full days. Passersby, including city personnel, had stopped to watch. Office folks had started taking their lunch there. A hotdog vendor had moved three blocks to take advantage of the crowd. It was a prime example of Chicago's right hand not knowing what the left hand was doing. It was finished before anyone realized what had happened.

He might have gotten away with it but he was so proud of it that he signed his initials to it. That might have even flown for awhile but being a loyal member of the Folks Nation, he added his gang affiliation sign, too. There was some brief news coverage but the Mayor's office put a stop to that real quick. And there was a neighborhood petition effort getting started to urge City Hall to keep it but it was too little, too late. That something like that could go on right under their noses was an embarrassment to the administration and they had acted quickly.

Knowing what was in store for him that next week, no one had any problem with his taking the fourth ticket. Or if there was a problem, it was silenced quickly by some of his 'bros'. You know, I've heard every awful thing that can be said about gangs and gang members, particularly the African American and Hispanic ones. And I've read all the statistics and studies. I know a lot of their activities fall outside of the law, but within their own organizations they hold truer to their set of ethics, values and laws than society in general ever thought of doing. And I respect that. They have great organizing and recruitment skills and very good business sense. My goal was always to simply channel all that energy and ability into something legal and without weapons. It was an uphill battle, though, when their higher ups were better connected with half the cops and politicians in the city than I was.

I gave them all their tickets and we settled on just meeting up there. They may have been only teenagers to most people and I called them 'my kids' but they had been functioning like adults since they were nine or ten years old. Organizing any event like your basic school fieldtrip would have been insulting. I'd learned early on that regardless of our good relationship, insulting them could be anything from alienating to downright dangerous.

I went by the house to change clothes and hang out, maybe at least *see* Marissa. By six thirty when she wasn't home I started to get worried. She'd been getting home at five o'clock almost religiously for the past week or so. She'd said she was a homebody and didn't socialize in the evenings. Most of her friends were co-workers or worked downtown and they stayed connected by having lunch together regularly. I hung around until I was almost late for the game. Still no Marissa, which worried me more.

Okay, okay. I wasn't worried for her safety. She grew up there. She was safer than I ever could be. I was worried I wouldn't see her. All right, and that she wasn't missing me like I was her. *And* that she might have a date. Satisfied? Now wipe that smirk off your face and let me get on with my story. Damn, I hate it when you do that.

I didn't pay too much attention to the game. I found a pay phone and called her number at half time. No one was home. The game went into overtime. Twice. By the time I got home it was after midnight. Still no Marissa. At that point I *was* getting worried for her well being. I lay down on the couch so I could hear her when she came in. I wasn't going to panic unless she didn't show for brunch. When she wasn't in at four in the morning my concern turned towards anger. I dealt with that for a while and finally drifted off to sleep.

18

I woke up right before eight o'clock to the sound of CATS on the stereo and her bebopping through her side of the house singing along. I got back in touch with my anger rather quickly. The more she sang the more it pissed me off. I knew I had to get over feeling like that but I couldn't seem to stop it. I just kept getting this picture in my head of some guy she barely knew with his hands all over her. I kept telling myself I was lucky she hadn't brought him home. Or maybe he was the lucky one. I was reacting to it badly enough to make a fool out of myself. That's the point when I knew I had it for Marissa far worse than I thought I did. I channeled all my energy into cooking. I must have made every fancy brunch dish I knew of. 'I'll show her', I thought, 'he probably can't cook worth a damn'.

She sailed through the door at precisely ten o'clock with a bottle of champagne and a gallon of orange juice for Mimosas. She looked like a million bucks and I looked like the slob that I was who had been up half the night pacing the floor like an idiot. I wanted to play it cool but my mouth ran away with me.

My hands went to my hips like an overly authoritarian parent. "So, I see you were going to just prance in here pretty as you please after staying out all night."

I must have really looked the part since she said, "Oh, gee, I guess I'm grounded, huh?" She went on through to the kitchen and got glasses. "Last

I heard, I was invited unless you're now planning on eating all that by yourself. And where do you get off monitoring my comings and goings?"

"For your information I was worried sick. I didn't have any idea where you were." My god, I thought, when did I turn into my mother? But at least I wasn't standing there slapping a belt in my hand like my father.

"I didn't know I was supposed to leave my itinerary with you."

"You could have left a note or something."

"Well, I'm sorry! I didn't realize we had progressed to the note leaving stage."

I leaned against the doorway into the kitchen. "Well, I hope you enjoyed yourself. Was he worth staying out all night for?"

"That was low, but as a matter of fact, he was. Or maybe I should say *they* were." At that she marched by me into the dining room shoving a full glass in my hand as she went by.

I stomped after her and sat down at the table. "They!!?"

"That's right," she said as she joined me. "All three of them. My guys know how to show a girl a good time. I may not do it often but when I do, I do it right. And I *always* stay all night."

"*Three*! Jeez, that's downright disgusting." I passed her the home-made Belgian waffles.

She reached for the fresh blueberry compote. "And by the way, Alex, did you have a good time at the game?"

"The game? How'd you know I went to the game?" I forked a piece of caramelized Virginia ham onto my plate.

"Because while I was helping my mother do the dishes my brother yelled from the living room, 'Hey sis, there's that nigger loving neighbor of yours.' Seems he saw you in a crowd shot." She pointed at the egg and peppers soufflé.

"You were, ah, at your folks' house?"

"Yes." She pointed again at the soufflé since I was holding it in mid-air.

"And the three guys were your brothers and your Dad?"

"Uh huh."

"Oh." I finally handed her the eggs and drank half my Mimosa in a single gulp.

I ate in sheepish silence for a few minutes. "Well, you still could have left a note."

"I see. And have you promoted yourself to my protector now?"

"Uh, yeah, something stupid like that."

"I don't need protecting Alex. I've got two brothers who I'm trying to wean off of that now."

I must have looked awfully dejected sitting there with my head hanging, stubbing the toe of my shoe on the hardwood floor. She leaned over and lifted my chin up with her finger. "But it was very sweet of you to be concerned. Misplaced and bordering on jealous, but sweet."

I know I turned beet red. Which was probably good. With any luck it was covering up what was left of the earlier green that she had just so astutely pointed out. "I, uh, wasn't jealous. I was, well… worried. What was I supposed to think? You were out all night. That's not like you. And you were singing this morning. That's *really* not like you."

"Alex, I was happy. I get like that on rare occasions. Well, actually not so rare lately." She looked away for a second and cleared her throat like she had just given away a secret. "I had a good time with my family for a change. They're no different, but I seem to be, and I was able to enjoy myself. I was looking forward to breakfast with you. Which by the way is delicious. And I was glad we'd made it past a Friday without a fight or an emotional catastrophe. I didn't realize that we were simply postponing it until this morning."

"Touché. I deserved that."

"Yes, you did. But I've been thinking about this all week and I've come to the conclusion that our problem lies in the pre-planned time we spend together. Every time we plan ahead something goes wrong. It's like we anticipate it to the point that we're on edge when it happens. Of course, you usually start it…"

"I start it!?"

"Yes, you do. You're the button pusher and I'm the reactor."

"More like the runner awayer."

"Whatever. But I didn't run this morning now did I?" She stopped and thought a moment. "But then, this morning you were way off base. The other times you've been right on target and that's what scares me off. But you're getting me away from my point. My point was that this past week has been really nice. It felt almost like having someone else in the house rather than living next door to someone. I thought maybe we could try something and see how it works. I was thinking we might try leaving the door open. Of course, we'd have to establish some boundaries. For instance, the extra bedroom where I paint and my bedroom and bath are strictly off limits unless you're invited. Got it?"

I didn't want to screw this up so I decided to try and process where it was coming from later. "Got it. Same here. My workout room, bedroom and bath, sacred space, invitation only. One other thing for me, though. You've got to show me you understand all my electronic gadgets before you use them."

"Fair enough. And if we want time by ourselves we say so up front."

"OK, and disagreements on TV shows result in each person going to their separate TV rooms."

"But you've got the big TV." She was so cute when she pouted.

"All right, we'll negotiate show by show as to who goes where. However, football games require the big screen. Good enough?"

"Good enough. Oh, and nobody eats the last of the other person's anything without permission."

"And rules to be amended as necessary." I held out my hand.

"Sounds good." She shook it.

We both sat there letting it all sink in. I needed someone to draw me a map because I sure as hell didn't know how we'd gotten to where we were. All I knew was that Marissa had suddenly decided to drive the car.

19

We finished breakfast, washed dishes and took strawberries and heavy cream and fresh Mimosas to the living room. It was Saturday morning still, so I flipped on cartoons. Marissa rolled her eyes but said nothing so I compromised and turned the sound way down. At least they were classic Looney Tunes and not the new, inane, mutant super heroes.

Marissa picked a magazine off the coffee table and idly flipped through it until she finally said, "So, let's talk about you for a change. You're always talking about my suit of armor, what about yours? What's with the knight in shining armor routine?"

"I don't know what you're talking about."

"Yes you do. I'm not saying it's put on or insincere. On the contrary, it's you through and through. I just wondered if you realized it. You even say things like 'accepting the gauntlet that's been thrown down before me'. People don't talk like that."

"Do one thing for me," I asked and she nodded. "Promise me that you'll remember when this conversation is over that you wanted to know." She nodded again.

"Would you believe I *was* a knight in a past life?"

"I can believe that *you* believe that. I've seen the titles in your personal library, remember?"

"You're the one that just said it was me through and through. You see, I believe everybody's soul has a basic character or nature. You carry that with you lifetime after lifetime trying to perfect it. So…"

"So you're trying to be the perfect knight?"

"No, no, no. Basic soul nature isn't that specific. That's just what I ended up being because it was natural for me during that time period."

"I knew I'd be sorry I asked. First of all, there's only ever been one person that came back. And he was *resurrected* not reincarnated. He came back as himself."

"Baa, baa, baa."

"Baaa?"

"Yeah, like sheep. Just accepting what they feed you and allowing yourself to be led around without question. Ever thought that maybe Jesus was just a man in his last of many incarnations and had reached spiritual perfection so that he was able to ascend at the time of his physical death? And having reached the level of an ascended master he was able to come back in any form he wanted to, so he chose *that* one because he wanted to be recognized in order to deliver the message that anyone who strives hard enough over enough lifetimes could achieve the same thing? He wasn't some martyr that died to wash away the sins of all future human beings. He was trying to show us that the power is within each and every one of us. That we are accountable to *ourselves* for every thought, act and behavior because until we get it right we just keep coming back over and over and over again. The Church twisted it all around because they saw a prime opportunity for mass social control. You've got to remember, Jesus wasn't a Christian yet he was one of the purest, most perfect men to ever walk this earth. Blind Christianity does not a good man make."

"Holy shit, Alex! You just undermined the whole foundation of the Church and my entire religious belief system in one breath."

"Frighteningly easy, isn't it?"

"I can't listen to any more of this."

"Okay, I'll get off religion and back to me, if you still want to hear it."

"All right, but hurry up and get back to *this* lifetime, please."

"If I have a certain basic soul nature, then over lifetimes I'm not just trying to perfect myself in an overall spiritual manner but I'm also trying to perfect my own personal nature. You with me? Good. If my basic nature is that of helper or saver then there are obvious good and healthy ways to be that and wrong, unhealthy ways. Right?"

"I can go along with that for argument's sake."

"The ultimate healthy helper or saver would be one who assists others in their growth without interfering in it, who gives guidance rather than directions, who does *with* not *for*, and is totally selfless in the entire endeavor. Rescuing on the other hand is unhealthy. It takes away the other person's personal power, makes them dependent and is a very selfish act. Rescuers are in it to get the adoration of the rescued. Make sense?"

"So far. You don't ever have a short simple answer do you?"

"No, but you didn't ask a simple question either. Knights were rescuers. I know because I was there, remember?" I couldn't help that and it did get a smile. "Yes, they were honorable, trustworthy, loyal, brave, self sacrificing etc. etc. But what kept them going was the admiration and adoration of the damsels and the public at large. That's not selfless. If they had done everything in complete secrecy just for the rightness of it and nothing else, that would have been selfless. But instead, they were showoffs."

"Alex, this is very interesting but could you get back to the here and now? You're making my head hurt."

"Oh all right. You asked about the knight in shining armor routine. It's just that. I seem to be stuck in that mode. It's my biggest karmic struggle. I can't seem to master the selflessness. I like to think I've carried the other helper/saver/knightly traits with me, among them honesty, trustworthiness, loyalty, bravery, but that damn rescuing mentality seems to come with it. The damsel in distress scenario really kicks it in."

"Well, I am no damsel so don't try to rescue me from anything."

"Don't worry. I gave up damsels after the last one."

"Was that the one who was living with you when you first moved in the brownstone?"

"Ah, you noticed me four years ago. How touching."

"Hard not to. The two of you were so mismatched it was pathetic. Talk about a sheep. She didn't last long either, if I remember correctly. Tell me about her."

"Why don't I just give you my basic, pitiful relationship scenario. It'll save me from having to tell you about each one individually." She shrugged. "Here goes: Alex discovers damsel in distress; Alex helps damsel escape mean stepfather, incestuous brother, sadistic boyfriend, abusive husband. Ad infinitum ad nauseum. Alex and damsel become friends; damsel becomes dependent; Alex falls in love; damsel feels obligated and tries to return that love; rocky relationship ensues; hideous breakup; broken heart; curtain. My grad professor called it the messiah complex. Said it happens all the time in the helping profession. Told us to recognize it for what it is and don't get sucked in by it. I've fallen victim to it four times so far so I guess he'd say my learning curve is flat."

"If it's any consolation, when I was a defense attorney before I started with the city, I got involved with two of my clients after I'd saved them from themselves."

"Very unethical, Counselor." I raised an eyebrow.

"No more than you." She raised her glass and clinked it with mine.

"True. This last one cured me though. When she left it was more a sense of relief than a broken heart. I haven't even dated since."

"Alex, that's got to be more than three years!"

"It's not been too bad. I'm not really a dater anyway. I'm part of that dying breed that actually wants a lifelong committed relationship. For better or worse and all that jazz. I got tired of the serial monogamy game. I'm not doing it again unless it's a forever thing. I'd rather be alone."

"She really must have done a number on you. Come on, tell me the story." She kept pushing my leg with her foot trying to goad me into it.

I poured us both another drink and told her to get comfortable.

20

"Her name was Jessie. Tupelo, Mississippi, my hometown and the birth-place of Elvis wasn't big enough to support a Rape Crisis Center, Domestic Violence Shelter, Homeless Soup Kitchen and other public assistance agencies separately so they lumped them all together in an old rundown fertilizer plant near the Downtown Mall. I'd always thought it was the perfect location for the General Crisis Center. Still dealing with the bullshit except this time it was the government's and society's and not the bull's. The government's because it refused to put enough time and money into preventing the social ills that brought the hollow eyed spiritless souls to the center; society's because it chose to look the other way.

It was Mother's Day weekend and I had offered to pull the forty-eight hour live-in counselor's shift so Kelly could take her family to the annual Gum Tree festival. I wasn't much for arts and crafts and I rel-ished the quiet of the center on the weekends. Not to mention the fact that it established a legitimate excuse for not attending our traditional all day family gathering honoring Big Momma, 102 that year and still mean as a buzzard.

On weekends the center maintained the crisis hotline, served two hot meals a day and supervised the shelter residents. Except during meals, which required the help of volunteers, the responsibilities were not too demanding for a solitary counselor.

That Sunday evening, on the way to help with the last meal, I happened to notice a small pudgy face peering in the glass front doors which opened into the Crisis Center's main reception area. I figured it was one of the neighborhood kids looking for a handout. But as I walked towards the doors the cherubic looking little face went through a dramatic transformation into the bruised and swollen face of a petite young woman somewhere in her early twenties.

And behind her I could see a fire engine red pickup barreling across the parking lot headed straight for the front steps. There was just enough time to yank the woman inside, and instruct her to lock the door behind me and call the cops, before the pickup jumped the curb and came to rest halfway up the stairs. A bumper sticker that claimed 'they can have my gun when they pry my cold dead fingers off it' was staring me in the face.

The guy got out of the truck and said, 'I want my wife you little shit'. Now I'm not little by regular standards but this guy was a monster. Two seventy-five, three hundred pounds at least. Big beefy arms, no neck, huge beer gut. Red faced and sweating like a hog. I was straining to hear the sirens from the police station right around the corner, when I chanced a look back through the locked front doors and realized the wife had slumped to the floor in the foyer in a daze.

I'm thinking 'great, no one knows we're here and I don't recall taking a course called Handling Irate Bubbas'. So I figured the first thing to do is to keep something substantial between him and me. Like the truck. And then to say something calming like "She's a little upset right now. Why don't you come back in an hour or so to pick her up?" Anything to get him to go away so I can get back inside.

He slammed his meaty fist on the hood of the truck, paused briefly to be sure he didn't leave a dent and said, "I'm the one who's a little upset, you little fuck, and I want her in this truck yesterday or your ass is mine!" He lunged at me and we started a slow waltz around the truck.

As I inched my way around in a complete circle I got to the open driver's door and saw the blue steel of a pistol sitting on the dash above the steering wheel. I figured if we kept it up he would make it back around to this point and then, I'm dead. The truck was still running and the passenger door was locked so I took a deep breath, dove, hit the lock button on the driver's door and slammed it shut. I took off running across the parking lot and around to the back door of the center.

By the time I made it back through the hallways to the front doors I could see Bubba standing outside and looking more like a big baby about to tune up for a good cry than a charging rhino. He'd lost all interest in his wife and could do little more than stare through the doors at me with his bottom lip quivering ever so slightly.

He whined, "What'd you go and do that for? I ain't got another set of keys on me. She's gonna overheat any minute now. Brand new engine'll be ruint to hell".

I reached over to the coat rack and held a coathanger up against the inside glass of the door. He was desperate but like any redneck worth his weight in salt, begging was out of the question. But trading wasn't. A good trade was a sign of Southern manhood. I could see a very dim bulb come on over his head.

He said, "Okay, I'll tell you what. She ain't been nothin' but trouble since the day her daddy give her to me anyway. So I'll give you Jessie there, free and clear, for that there coathanger. What d'ya say?"

That he thought of her as an object that could be traded away was sickening but I knew it would work so I unlocked one door and cracked it open slightly and said, "You never set foot on this property again. You never lay a hand on her again. She's not yours anymore. And she gets everything in the house that belongs to her."

He mumbled, "You got it. No problem. Sure. Now toss it here, quick".

I decided to push it, "*And* you say you're sorry".

He started in with an, "Aw, c'mon".

"I mean it!" I yelled. "She's gonna blow if you don't". I pointed at the truck.

"All right, all right", he hollered, "I am".

"You are what?"

"Sorry. I'm sorry. Now give me the goddamned coathanger".

So I tossed it out the door, locked it back and turned around to see if yet another thrown away person could bring herself back from the edge. From there on you can just apply my basic relationship formula and fill in the blanks. Of course there is one small difference. Even though it was a good while from the time she was a client to the time when we started our involvement it was still a huge scandal. Seems Bubba, actually his name was Darnell, was related to the Sheriff who was related by marriage to the Mayor who was my ultimate boss. I was asked to resign, my family was mortified, and I basically got run out of town on a rail. So I found the director's job at the Teen Center here and brought her with me."

Marissa was slowly shaking her head in disbelief. "So what happened to her?"

"She eventually went back to Bubba. He *did* offer to buy her a double wide, after all, if she'd come back."

"Double wide?"

"Mobile home."

"Oh. I'm sorry Alex, that must have hurt."

"It was a relief actually." I forced myself to grin real big and say in the redneck voice I'd been using, "Hell, she'd been nothin' but trouble from the day Bubba give her to me anyway."

"Alex! That's awful!" She thwacked me with the magazine she still had in her hand. Then we both started laughing.

"You gotta laugh to keep from crying, so they say," I said as I wiped tears from the corners of my eyes.

21

We spent the rest of the afternoon like that. Regaling each other with horror stories of failed relationships, high school puppy loves, dates from hell. When we tired of that we fixed sandwiches, got chips and beers and settled in to watch a movie. She picked Wuthering Heights out of my collection. I laid on the couch and she curled up in the big, overstuffed armchair.

When I woke up I had a blanket over me, the TV was off and she had the floorlamp on and was reading in the chair. It was dark outside. I lay there feigning sleep, with my eyes half open watching her. In all the discussion earlier about relationships I had kept us away from describing our dream person, as those discussions are wont to go in that direction sometimes. I knew if we got on the subject I might tell her she was it, in a moment of weakness.

I must have drifted back off into a great daydream because I lost my sense of continuity and pictured things that I tried very hard *not* to think about when I was awake. When I woke up the second time I must have moved because she was looking my way. I smiled and said, "Hey."

"Hi there, sleepyhead. That must have been some dream."

I let that one go and said, "Sorry I fell asleep on you."

"Don't be. You're kind of cute when you're asleep."

"Oh, and I'm not otherwise?" I stretched and yawned and propped up on one elbow. I could feel my hair sticking up on the crown of my head.

"I didn't say that."

I started thinking about that map again and how we had arrived at this point. "I'm surprised you're still here."

"I like it over here."

"You do, do you?"

"This isn't going to come out right and I apologize ahead of time, but it has kind of a lived in, 'guy quality' to it that makes me feel like I can relax and put my feet on the furniture."

"Kind of high class Salvation Army decor?"

"Yeah. No. Oh, you know what I mean."

We sat in comfortable silence yet again. I was beginning to believe this house sharing was going to work out. She must have finished a chapter because she marked it and put her book down. She turned towards me with a serious look on her face. "I hate to talk business on a weekend but the judge in that graffiti case…"

"Work of art case."

"Okay, work of art. He contacted me personally last week to see if I'd started my community service. I'll be honest, when it first happened I called in some favors and tried to get it dropped or changed but he wouldn't hear of it. He was quite pleased with himself during that whole mess. So I've arranged to take off this next week, that is, if you'll still have me." She batted her eyes at me in over exaggerated flirtation.

.It worked. Until I had an awful thought. What if all the niceness and sweetness today was just a ploy to have me go easy on her? 'Stop it', I told myself, 'that's the style of women in your past. It's not Marissa. Today was real'. I decided to tread lightly and said, "Sure."

"Good. I feel better about it now that I've gotten to know you. I'm still a little nervous but I don't think you'll throw me to the wolves like I thought you would at first. I know you'll make me work hard. I can see it in your eyes. But that's all right I can handle it. It might even be fun. I've been wanting to see what you do all day. You don't talk about it much."

"Sometimes it's rough enough the first time around and you don't want to spend any downtime reliving it, know what I mean?" She nodded. "I've learned to leave most of it there when I come home and pick it back up when I go in the next day. You should probably know that so you'll understand that when I come home in a real funk it's something major and I just need to be left alone. Then there are the occasional days where it's nothing but laughs and fun and success stories. You have to grab on to those and hang on tight. They don't happen too often. You'll see."

"So, what kinds of things will I be doing?"

"I don't know yet. I didn't think you'd go through with it to tell the truth. It would probably do you good to experience it all. But I'll have to give it some thought. Do you know how to dress knife wounds?"

Her eyes got so huge I burst out laughing. "I'm kidding. Not that you won't see any but they go to the clinic next door."

"You lead a strange life, Alex."

"I know. It's that saver in me."

It must have been something she needed to sleep on because she immediately started yawning. It was getting late and we said good night. It sure felt good to leave that door open.

22

I got up the next morning and found a note taped to the end of the hallway.

> A-
>
> Figured we'd made it to the note leaving stage now.
> Gone to early Mass then to Mama and Pop's for
> lunch. Will be home later this afternoon. See you
> then.
>
> -M

I piddled around the house, read and took a nap. I woke up from my nap with the greatest idea. I brainstormed on it to see if I could actually pull it off and decided it was possible.

By the time Marissa got home I was bouncing off the walls. We went out for Chinese and ended up seeing a movie, too. When we got back she was still trying to pry it out of me. All I would tell her was that I had decided on her community service work, that she should get a good night's sleep, dress warmly in clothes she didn't mind ruining and be ready to leave with me at seven o'clock sharp.

She was ready to go on time the next morning and we headed straight for City Hall. I had a Polaroid camera with me and had to stop in the middle of rush hour traffic to get the very best shot of the mural. I managed to get three pictures before getting threatened with bodily harm if I didn't get going. I found a place to park and we went looking for Carlos. We found him sitting under one of the landscaping trees staring at his masterpiece. I knew him well enough to know that he probably planned on doing that all week and then painting over it on Friday. He could knock it out in one day with a roller. Not much art in painting something a solid color.

I handed him the pictures and he seemed appreciative. Then he looked at Marissa and back at me and pulled me aside. "What's she doin' here, man?"

I brought him back over to Marissa. "Allow me to introduce you. Carlos, this is Marissa Scafidi, attorney for the City of Chicago, and your personal assistant for the week. Marissa, this is Carlos Diaz, avant garde artiste and your community service work supervisor."

They both looked at me like I had lost my mind. "The only catch is that I get to choose the project."

"Hey, Mac, I already got a project, you know."

"You and I both know you can knock that out on Friday. They did-n't give you hours they gave you a task. Marissa here, on the other hand, got hours. Forty of them."

"And I get to boss her around for all of them?"

Marissa looked at me like she wanted to kill me. "Both of you just hold on. You've got to trust me on this. Yes, Carlos, you are her super-visor for the whole forty hours. And I imagine you'll be a pain in the ass at first because you think she has somehow personally wronged you just by doing her job. But my hope is that you'll end up working as a team and maybe even like each other by the end of the week. It would mean a lot to me if that happened. Because in case you're too damned hard headed to see it, I care a lot about the both of you." And with that unex-pected self-revelation I turned and headed back to the Jeep.

Their footsteps fell in behind me and I heard Carlos say, "Hell, I knew Mac liked me but how'd you get in the picture? There somethin' I need to know 'bout here?"

"Don't start with me, Carlos. I don't like this any better than you do." Marissa snapped.

"Hey, don't be tellin' me 'bout myself. I be likin' this fine. Just fine."

When they got to the Jeep they argued over who would ride up front. Carlos won when he told her that if she continued to get uppity with him he was going to write her up. Marissa scrunched into the back seat. If this didn't end up working out the way I envisioned it I knew I was going to pay for it for a very long time *if* she ever spoke to me again.

I drove directly to the closest paint store and parked. I told Carlos to take one of the photos in with them and get all the paint they would need to recreate the mural. And I handed him my credit card.

"No shit! Mac are you for real? Wait a minute, what's this ya'll shit?"

"Just what I said. The two of you are going to recreate that mural on the side of the Teen Center."

"I don't work with nobody."

"You do now."

23

After a big hullabaloo with the store owner accusing Carlos of having stolen my credit card and Marissa trying to vouch for him and my finally having to come in and sign for it myself and blessing out the guy for his bigoted stereotyping, we were on our way.

When we got to the Center, Carlos made a big show in front of his buddies of ordering Marissa around. They all lined up against the outside wall that was to be his canvas for the week and hooted and catcalled while she unloaded the Jeep until I ushered them all inside for their GED class.

That was one of my strictest rules. If you hung out at the Center during school hours you had to be doing something learning related. Most of those kids had been kicked out of school for behavior problems but it didn't mean they were stupid, just unable to function well in highly structured environments. The ones that came during those hours really wanted to learn something. Others intentionally avoided me like the plague until after school hours were up. That actually made things a whole lot easier since everyone there at least had one thing in common. They had the desire to learn. Any other shortcomings could be worked out. Everybody worked individually and at their own pace on their GED curriculums in the morning. Good work was rewarded with time in the computer lab to surf the Internet as they pleased. Good behavior was rewarded with points on a weekly scorecard.

After lunch, the afternoon was devoted to dissecting the latest movies, music or art for their messages and values, content and structure. I usually sat in on that as a much-needed break from doing individual counseling and crisis intervention all morning. The discussions were intense to say the least. An organization called One Hundred Black Men, which actually had about five hundred members, kept me supplied with tutors and mentors and provided great male role models that most of those kids didn't have in their lives.

I stuck out like a sore thumb being the only white person for miles around. When the all minority Board of Directors had hired me four years previously they were very upfront about the fact that I was a token director, a strategy to keep the majority white city administration and community off their backs and out of their business. I had no powers, no say in anything and was basically told to stay out of the way.

Not having anything else to do, I started writing grants, which the Board didn't have time to do. I got a little respect when the money started flowing for new programs and staff. When I pulled off a half million dollar capital campaign to completely renovate the old warehouse where we were located, the community finally began to embrace me and let me in. I was still 'that crazy honky' but I was beginning to be *their* crazy honky. That was my first two years.

One of the biggest challenges after that was getting the African American and Hispanic communities to cooperate with each other. The Center was right on the border between the two neighborhoods. I'd never thought about there being prejudice between minority groups so it was a real eye opener for me to find that the African American community felt they had complete ownership of the Center and didn't want to let the Hispanic community in. Building that bridge took the next two years. The relationship was tenuous at times but it was there. If it hadn't been, Carlos, who was mixed race, would have never been allowed to paint that mural on the Center.

I wandered into my office, sat down at my desk and looked up to see Marissa standing in the doorway.

"Alex, this is not going to work."

"Sure it is."

"No. It's not. First of all, all he bought was spray paint. You can't paint with that. You don't have enough control over it. Secondly, the wall is brick. It's not even a flat surface. And he won't listen to anything I tell him."

"Then quit trying to tell him anything. You're supposed to be taking directions from him. Quit trying to exercise your majority mentality. Lighten up. You might learn something."

"Ooooohhhh, I hate you." She turned on her heel and stomped out.

I just smiled. That didn't hurt too much since I knew there was a *very* fine line between love and hate.

I pulled out some files and had just gotten them spread across my desk when Carlos barged in.

"Mac, this ain't gonna work."

"Sure it is."

"No, man, it's not. She won't listen to anything I tell her. She keeps saying it can't be done. Man, I did City Hall didn't I? It looked good, didn't it?"

"Yes it did. And this is your chance to learn some people management skills. Quit trying to be a bad ass. Try giving directions instead of orders. She's actually a very accomplished artist herself. Lighten up. You might learn something."

"Ah, man, this sucks!" And he stomped out.

I just smiled. I love it when a plan comes together.

24

I went out at lunch to see if they'd killed each other yet. They were huddled together on the sidewalk over a big piece of paper. When I got closer I realized they'd taken one of the table covers out of the lunch area and were sketching on it. I turned to look at the wall and saw that they had already finished a vague outline of all the components of the picture.

Carlos ran over to me. "Hey Mac, we gonna need more paint."

"More paint! You've hardly gotten started."

"Yeah, but we gonna add highlighting and shading and shit to make it more, uh, three dimensional."

"*We* are?"

"Yeah, me and Scafidi. Hey, did you know I got a good sense of composition and dimensions?"

"You've got a good sense about more than that," I said as I clapped him on the back and we walked over to Marissa.

She stood up and pulled me aside. "He's a very talented young man, Alex. We need to see if we can get him into some classes to hone his natural ability. I'll even pay for them."

I opened my mouth but all that wanted to come out was 'I love you' so I shut it again and just stood there nodding, thinking.

I got my composure back and said, "Why pay for them when you could teach him yourself?"

"Me!?"

"Yes you. You're good. Very good. And you've had classes haven't you? Teach him what you know. If he wants to go further with it after that we'll send him where he needs to go. But right now, he'd probably have trouble adjusting to your basic white, middle class Art 101 setting."

"Maybe you're right. I could show him a few things. Teach him some new mediums. Stuff like that." She turned to look at the two-story brick wall and smiled. "Maybe how to work on a smaller scale, too. I hate that extension ladder."

"Hold off saying anything to him until y'all have finished this project. By then you'll both know if you can transition to teacher and student."

"Good idea. Now what's for lunch? I'm starving!"

"Let's see. I think it's chittlins, greens and pig's ear sandwiches," I said as I walked her back to Carlos.

"That sounds awful."

"Actually, they're pretty good. But no one's going to make you eat soul food on your first day. I think it's ham sandwiches, chips and a pickle."

I handed her my credit card and keys to the Jeep. "When ya'll are through with lunch go get whatever you need."

"You *are* getting reimbursed for this aren't you? We already spent almost two hundred dollars this morning and this trip should be about as much again."

"This isn't in the Center's budget. But don't worry about it. It keeps me in the Salvation Army decor to which you've become accustomed."

By the end of the day the mural was beginning to take on the likeness of the original. When we got home Marissa went in the house, ate a bowl of cereal and went straight to bed saying every muscle in her body hurt from keeping a deathgrip on the ladder, not to mention climbing up and down and moving it a hundred times. She and Carlos were getting along fine but he was making her work for it.

The rest of the week went well. Just as they did at City Hall, people started gathering to watch the progress. However, it was done in the style of the neighborhood, which was far different and a lot more fun than the stuffed shirts downtown. Of course we were downtown, too, but as Tyrone liked to say, we were in 'downtown browntown'. Folks brought lawn chairs and boom boxes. Someone brought a barbecue pit made from a hundred-gallon drum. The local mom and pop grocer donated racks of ribs. It was spontaneous community pride at its best. When they would put the finishing touches on a section everyone would cheer Carlos. By late Wednesday they even started acknowledging and speaking to Marissa.

The last 'spray stroke' occurred around four o'clock Thursday afternoon. Carlos forgot himself and hugged his co-artist. It was magnificent. It put the smaller one at City Hall to shame. That's what an expense account at the paint store will do for you. When you're stealing it you don't have near the color selection.

Carlos signed his initials on the bottom right corner. He knew better than to try the gang insignia. Nothing gang related was allowed in or near the Center. He turned and handed the can to Marissa. She just stood there frozen in place. Carlos nudged her and said, "Go on. I want you to. It's yours, too."

Marissa looked back over her shoulder at me with tears in her eyes. She knew I was the only one who understood what the real holdup was. I nodded and mouthed 'do it'. She walked up to the wall and with a deep breath signed her initials under Carlos'. The crowd cheered for both of them.

She was on cloud nine the whole way home. "I know I haven't seen the down side of it yet, but I think I have a better idea why you do what you do. Why you fight for it and believe in it so much. Why you're so passionate about it."

"They're good kids, they just don't have much else in their lives. You've got to remember that the ones that come to the Center, while not perfect, are trying. It's the ones who don't come that worry me."

25

Friday was a little bit different experience for her. I hated for her to end her time on a down note but I wanted her to see it all. We started with a home visit to check on one of my favorites. Lavon was seventeen years old and had been shot in the head on Valentine's Day with his own gun by his fifteen-year-old sister because he was making fun of her 'nappy' hair. She was in the detention center, he couldn't even tie his own shoelaces anymore and his mother was on crack. He'd been the bread-winner in the family, albeit selling dope, but now his mother was pissed at him for 'going and getting shot'. So she refused to help him. His gang brothers made regular visits to be sure he'd eaten and had clean clothes and to help him take a shower.

I pushed the door to the apartment open and walked in announcing our arrival as I went. 'Mom' was passed out on the couch and stunk of urine. I ignored her and went to the back bedroom to tell Lavon we were there and ask if he needed anything. He just shrugged his shoulders. Marissa walked up behind me as I was slipping a folded twenty under the lamp on the bedside table. If his mother found it she'd just smoke it up. I introduced them and then headed back the way we came to do some work. I started cleaning and picking up in the living room and Marissa followed my lead and went into the kitchen. Lavon's bro's did a lot of things but cleaning wasn't one of them. I usually spent about an hour a week, which wasn't much, but it helped.

Marissa let out a scream when she went to the kitchen. I ran to see what was wrong but had guessed before I got there. I finally found her in the hall outside the apartment door. When I talked her down and got her back inside she went to the kitchen door and just pointed at the sink and a small table both piled high with dirty dishes and old food containers. There were several dozen cockroaches lazily munching on the remains, not the least bit concerned that the light had been turned on or that there was movement in the room. Suburban roaches scatter but ghetto roaches just stare at you. There were also large rat droppings on the kitchen counter. I reached way back on the top of the fridge and brought out a pair of rubber gloves. "Here, I got these a few weeks ago. It makes it a little easier." I also handed her a can of bug spray. "This won't make a dent in the overall population but it might make you feel better." And I left her to it.

When I finished with the living room it looked pretty decent. I'd picked up a full bag of trash, cleaned, dusted and vacuumed. Marissa'd done a better job in the kitchen than I'd ever had time to do. She looked a little green when she came out but she had survived. We were on a roll so I tackled the bathroom and Marissa straightened up in Lavon's room and talked to him while I finished up. He seemed to enjoy the company of a beautiful woman and just kept grinning at everything she said.

As we were leaving Marissa said, "Nobody should have to live like this."

"A lot do though. Some choose it," I nodded at the mother, "and some don't." I nodded towards Lavon's room. "They had it pretty good until the shooting. His sister kept the place spotless. Lavon brought in good money even though it was drug money. They had nice stuff. His record was clean somehow and he had been accepted at the Community College in computer science. His mother's always been a druggie but the kids worked around it. He was going to get out of here and take his sister with him. Then this happened and Mom started pawning everything they had to keep herself supplied. When it was all gone she started turning tricks. They call it 'crack for crack.'"

"God, that's awful. So why do you do it? You can't give all your money away and you can't clean every apartment in the neighborhood. Why this one?"

"I don't know. He's special. He was a success story in the making. He was turning it around and it was snatched away from him."

Back at the Center I had three sessions in a row. Each one gave permission for Marissa to sit in with us once I convinced them she wasn't with Social Services. I had a pregnant fourteen year old who was torn between abortion and raising it herself. She was leaning towards the latter because she thought it would be nice to have something that had no choice but to love her. But on the other hand she didn't want to 'have no messed up baby' so she wanted to know what the odds were that it would be okay since its father was her brother.

The second one was a kid from some little podunk farming town about two hundred miles away who had come to see the big city. She'd been plucked right off the bus by a charming fellow named Andre who got her coked up, raped her and then put her on the street to work for him. When she didn't bring in enough money he beat her senseless and set her out in the gutter. She'd heard we could help her get home.

The third was a young man who took almost an hour of hemming and hawing and telling his life story only to find that his biggest concern at the moment was that he was afraid his penis was going to rot off.

Now that we have all the talk shows and the investigative reports on television, these stories aren't shockers to anybody anymore. Or at least that's what we think. But it's a very different experience when they're sitting next to you; their eyes pleading with you to do something and your knowing that if they don't get it from you they probably will quit looking.

I sent them all to eat and to sit in on the afternoon discussion group and then set about pulling strings at Families First, Traveler's Aid and the Walk-In Clinic. We ate in the office and then joined the discussion group. I gave our three clients their appointment times, directions, my business card and bus tokens as needed. Marissa was pretty shook up at that point. But hearing the group pick apart and discuss with great insight the movie "Like Water For Chocolate" seemed to give her some hope.

I thought we would just slide for the rest of the day so when the discussion group was over we sat in the bleachers and watched a pick up basketball game. Some of the girls were running the game clock and keeping score, so I could just sit back. Marissa was enjoying watching because by that time she knew most of the guys on the floor. Like me, she had her favorites but you tried not to show it.

One of hers was Antoine. In the third quarter someone came down hard on the bridge of his nose and he hit the floor. He managed to get up on all fours and was bleeding pretty badly. Everybody on the court scattered. I stood up and headed for my office. Halfway there somebody yelled, "Hey Mac!" I turned in time to see Marissa a few steps away from Antoine. He was trying like crazy to wave her off. She was shaking her finger at the others and chastising them, "What's the matter with you? Can't you see he's hurt?"

I yelled her name so loud it bounced back to me from the other side of the gym. She looked up, startled.

I yelled, "Stop. Right there. Just stay put."

"But…" She took another step.

I yelled, "NO!" Antoine was still trying to wave her away so she stood there completely confused.

I came running back with the first aid kit.

"What the hell's wrong with you? I was just going to help him," she snapped.

"He's positive," I said as I handed her latex gloves.

"He's what?"

"Antoine's HIV positive. That's why he was telling you to stay away. Put on the gloves."

She was a real trooper. She didn't hesitate but I had a sense she was getting ready to crack on the inside. She helped me get him cleaned up and pack his nose. It looked broken so I sent him next door to the clinic. I bleached the floor and disposed of everything in a biohazard bag. The game picked up where it left off.

She didn't start to visibly shake until just a few steps from the office door. I got her in, closed the door and closed the blinds.

"How…?"

"Dirty needle. Three years ago."

"I don't care about that."

"You better care about that."

"No. I mean how can you do this day in and day out?"

"Look around you Marissa. How can I not?"

26

Before we could get into that any further the phone interrupted us. It was the local ABC affiliate saying they wanted to set up a live interview for the Monday night local news at six o'clock. They'd heard about the mural and the story behind it and thought it would make a good human-interest piece. They wanted a guarantee on an exclusive saying not to be surprised if their competitors got wind of it and showed up unannounced. Which meant that any station could cover the story but no one but ABC could have an interview until after their six o'clock show was over. Always needing positive press, I agreed. They wanted the artists, myself and the President of the Board. That last one would be tricky since I hadn't yet told him what we'd done. I thought I might try to slide around that one.

I told Marissa the news when I got off the phone. She thought about it for a few minutes and said, "I'll do it."

"Was there any doubt?"

"At the beginning of the week I would have done anything to keep my family from knowing where I was and what I was doing. But not now. I'm proud of it. This week has crumbled a lot of that 'baa, baa, baa' belief system that was fed to me my whole life. I know it won't go away over night. It's pretty deeply entrenched. But I've got first hand experience to work from now and I'd like to keep coming back when I can. Do you take volunteers?"

"Well, well, well. Mission accomplished." I leaned back in my chair and laced my fingers behind my head.

"Fell right into it, didn't I?"

I grinned. "Hook, line and sinker."

"You do know my family will blame you for this. Mama and Pop won't be too bad but my brothers already hate you and this will simply add fuel to the fire."

"If I can deal with *my* family, I think I can deal with yours. But can you?"

"I've got to. It's about time I grew up and had a mind of my own."

"Hear, hear," I said. "Now let's go home."

One of the great things about that community was that you never had to put up flyers for an event. All you had to do was tell two people about it and everyone knew by nightfall. I put out the word about Monday night and we left. We drove by City Hall and Carlos was covering the last vestiges of his original. He didn't seem the least bit upset now. I told him about Monday night and he grinned from ear to ear and came over to do a high five. I put the Jeep in park so I could return the gesture except that he walked around to the passenger side and slapped hands with Marissa. Oh well, I thought, that's what I was aiming for all along.

It was supposed to be colder that weekend and it had been a hell of a week so we decided to pick up firewood and videos and just hole up for the next two days and recuperate.

27

"Alex?"

"Yeah, Sharon."

"Please, please, tell me you're at a stopping point."

"I can be. I didn't really want to talk about the next part anyway."

"Well you'll have to. But not now. It's three o'clock in the morning."

"Is it? I'm sorry. I should have warned you. Pain meds have the opposite effect on me than most people. They wire me up."

"I see that. And I'd forgotten you're propensity for remembering every detail about every thing. It's not normal."

"Is that your diagnosis, o'favorite shrink o'mine?"

"For now that's all I've got to go on. I almost wish they'd given you general anesthesia. Then we'd both be sleeping right about now. Are we going to get to the bullet wound in your butt anytime in the near future? Six hours and you're still in 1996."

"All in good time, Sharon, all in good time. I'll shut up for now. Do me a favor, though. If you see Marissa before I do, tell her I love her."

"Oh, I will. That's the only thing so far that's perfectly clear."

"I hope so. I sure as hell hope so."

"Goodnight Alex. Get some sleep for God's sake."

Marissa

Part One

28

Tuesday June 8, 1999 10:00AM

"Marissa, come in, come in. Have a seat anywhere you like. Can I get you something to drink?"

"No thank you, Sharon, I'm fine. Well, obviously I'm not fine. What I meant to say is I'm not thirsty. Actually, I haven't been able to keep anything on my stomach since day before yesterday. I think it's nerves. I mean, I'm way past morning sickness. Not that I had much morning sickness. I was lucky in that respect. Some women get it really bad I hear. The little bit I did have Alex was such a sweetheart. Waited on me hand and foot. Made me stay in bed. But it wasn't bad. Just a little nausea. But you know Alex, always over reacting. Always over protective. But it really was sweet. Oh, God, I'm babbling aren't I? I'm sorry. I've never done this before. I need to shut up, don't I?"

"No, no. Marissa, you're fine. Just try to relax. Take a deep breath and get comfortable. This isn't the inquisition. No bright lights. No Chinese water torture. We're just going to talk. The past two days must have been very traumatic for you and I'm just here to help the two of you sort it out and get back on your feet. That's all."

"I know. I'm okay. Really I am. I've never been in therapy before. I'm just a little nervous, that's all. Alex says therapy is wonderful and that you're wonderful. I just never thought I'd be here. And certainly not under these circumstances. Maybe I wouldn't be here now if I'd gotten some help a long time ago. I never thought I needed it. But I guess I did since I keep screwing up this relationship. I keep thinking of Alex lying in that hospital bed and that it's all my fault. But then I always thought therapy was for crazy people. And I know I'm not crazy. Although, I realize now that thinking I could ever live without Alex, that I could ever be happy with someone else, was pretty crazy. So maybe I am. Or maybe not crazy but stupid, or weak. Do you think I'm weak? I mean, our relationship's not an easy one but how many are? Oh, God, I'm sorry. I'm doing it again, aren't I?"

"Marissa, it's all right. That's what we're here for. To figure it all out. Nobody's pointing fingers or laying blame and I want you to be careful not to do that to yourself. Okay? Can you do that for me? Good. Relationships *are* tough and I'm sure the two of you have some extra strikes against you that sometimes make it even more difficult but we can work through those obstacles if you both are committed to it. I have the advantage of knowing Alex very well. And I was in that hospital room till three a.m. this morning getting the beginnings of the unabridged story. But one thing that was clearly evident is the degree of commitment and depth of love that's there. Is it there for you, too?"

"Oh God, yes. *Yes.* I never thought it was possible. I always thought that loving like this was bull...uh, baloney. Most of the time I feel blessed, like the luckiest woman in the world. But it's so intense, sometimes I just feel scared and confused like I don't deserve it or can't handle it. Does that make any sense?"

"First of all, it's okay to say bullshit or anything else you feel like saying. This is a safe place for you and I *don't* have virgin ears, I assure you. Secondly, yes, that makes perfect sense. I have no doubt that a relationship with Alex can be very intense. Why don't we start at the beginning and work up to the point that you started feeling scared and confused?"

"You do know Alex, don't you? Problem is, I've felt scared and confused off and on since the beginning. Alex is so steady and our life together is incredible as long as I don't think about it too much.

Whenever I can just let go and feel my love, I'm okay. But then I start thinking and it all goes to heck, I mean hell."

"All right then. Let's do this. Start by telling me when you first realized how you *felt*."

29

When did I first realize how I felt? This is the therapy part, isn't it? Okay, deep breath. I suppose I need to face the fact that I've got to do this. That Alex and I both need to if we're going to salvage our relationship. I don't envy you, Sharon. You look exhausted. We've been together for three and a half years now and if there's one thing I know is that it takes Alex an eternity to tell a simple story and this one is way beyond simple.

Avoiding the subject? Well, yes, I suppose I am. Alex gives me a hard time about that, too. Okay, when did I first know how I felt? This isn't the first time I've heard that question. My parents accepted Alex at first because they thought we were just friends. You know, neighbors. That kind of stuff. I didn't think they could have handled it to know we were living together much less anything else. They're *too* Catholic. They didn't want me to be happy as much as they wanted me to be proper.

None of my friends accepted Alex. They'd started asking questions, diplomatic and polite at first. I was honestly indignant and categorically denied everything. But every time they asked or made snide comments it started me thinking about it. I didn't want to think about it so I spent less and less time around them. Which, in turn meant more and more time around Alex, which just made my feelings deeper and deeper. I told myself that I never lied to my friends and I never lied to my parents. I suppose I was too busy lying to myself.

With my parents I just listened very carefully to their questions and answered accordingly.

"Alex ever done anything, well, you know, er…inappropriate?"

"Inappropriate? *No* Pop, Alex has never been inappropriate."

"You're not dating anyone right now?"

"No Pop, I'm not dating right now."

"You need to find a nice Catholic boy, Marissa. Settle down."

"Settle down? Yes Pop, that's exactly what I want."

"Good, good. Glad to hear it. You're Mother'll be happy."

But it was emotionally exhausting trying to keep up appearances. They were constantly trying to fix me up with a one of those 'good Catholic boys from the neighborhood'.

Early on we were in the 'just friends' stage. Actually I kept it that way for the majority of a year. I guess you can tell I have trouble letting my feelings out. I'm an attorney. Not only because I'm good at it but also because it suits me. I get to stay in my head. I don't have to feel. Just convict. Maybe that's why I'm good at it. It's safe. Besides, why should I allow myself to fall for someone that no one else in my life seemed to like? It would have been much too difficult to fall in love with someone that my family and friends were uncomfortable around.

So we were just friends. Of course that was after we had waved the white flag and realized that we fought so much because it scared us how much we liked each other. As a matter of fact, we were getting along so well that about three or four months after we both moved into the duplex we actually discussed sharing one side and using the other side for office space since we both dreamed of starting our own practices. I bounced the idea off Mama and Pop once, emphasizing that it would be a *roommate* arrangement. Mama was appalled and Pop accused Alex of masterminding the whole scheme in order to 'get a foot in the door with me and try something funny'. So Alex's stuff stayed on Alex's side and my stuff stayed on my side. But we'd already been keeping the connecting door open so we could come and go as we pleased and treat it like one big house for more than a month, so we just kept it that way.

It's strange, now that I look back on it. Alex never was the first to suggest anything that would bring us closer, never pushed me to let down my walls any faster than I could. That unspoken responsibility lay on my shoulders. And I probably did it faster on my own than if I had been pressured into it.

It was a few weeks after we started leaving the door open that I recognized I might have feelings for Alex that transcended friendship. I wasn't sure where they came from. I certainly couldn't believe they were there. They didn't last long, though. I wouldn't let them. They scared me so badly that I stuffed them way, way down. I mean, Alex? God, it was still hard to believe we were friends. And becoming good friends at that. As far as I was concerned Alex represented everything I'd been taught to either hate, oppose or not believe in. It made for great repartee and heated debate. Both of which I thrive on. But attracted to? No way!

My friends said they knew it from the start because I constantly talked about that night in the elevator even though I swore it was the worst night of my life. In retrospect I can see it, too. There was a connection, a spark, the minute we laid eyes on each other. But the first time I began to even consider it was the day the rat died. Yes, I know, every other woman worries about the rabbit dying. But not me, with me, it's a rat.

30

It was a Saturday morning after I'd spent a wonderful but exhausting week doing community service work at the Teen Center that Alex ran. I was curled up on the couch in my living room watching C-Span. I thought I heard Alex moving around on the other side and sure enough in a few minutes two big slippered feet came shuffling through the connecting door. I said that coffee was ready in the kitchen and got a gruff mumble in return. I was just about to get up and fix some for myself when my favorite mug appeared over my shoulder. I must have spent a few too many seconds lost in my appreciation of being waited on. When I looked up C-Span was gone and Bugs Bunny was in its place.

I'd been hearing a strange scritching noise all morning coming from the direction of the fireplace. It happened again and we both jumped and looked in that direction. Alex got up and started looking for the source which is basically the way I had envisioned things going since I wasn't about to go poking around. I went to get a flashlight. I heard one of the glass fireplace doors squeak open, a loud 'Holy shit' and the door slam shut again. I ran back to the living room.

Alex plopped back down on the couch. "I think it's a rat."

"Is it a big rat?"

"It's too dark in there. I didn't get a good look but I think it's big."

"How big is big?"

"Big is as big does. If it breaks the glass, stomps to the kitchen and fixes breakfast then it's really, really big. If however, it goes quietly back up the chimney and out of our lives then it's not so big."

"God, you are such a smartass."

"Yes I am. And stop calling me God. Someone might hear you and then my secret will be out."

"I'm ignoring you. How long before he leaves? I want to build a fire."

"I don't think it's that easy. There's a lot of fire proofing material lying around in there. It looks like he's been trying to get out and can't."

I sat back down. "Oh great, the one thing that's helped me make it through this week is knowing that I could spend the entire weekend in front of a roaring fire being nothing more than a sofa vegetable."

"Couch potato. Well, I can get it out if you want me to."

"Oh, no. I'll get an exterminator over here. At least right now it's trapped in there. If you start fooling with it it's likely to get loose in the house."

So I went and started calling exterminators. The only one who could come that day wanted seventy-five dollars just to drive in the driveway on a Saturday. So I set up a time for the next week and went back to the living room to pout. After a while I decided that we could replace the roaring fire with junk food and perhaps still salvage the weekend. So I left Alex there and went to the grocery.

I got back about an hour later. I walked in and found Alex sitting in front of the fireplace with a great big jar I used for making sun tea on one side and a pellet gun on the other.

"What are you doing?" I had learned it was not a good idea to leave Alex unsupervised for any length of time.

"I had to kill it."

"Well good, I'm glad it's dead. But I thought I told you to leave it alone."

"An exterminator would have killed it right off the bat. I tried to save it."

"Oh, that's right, I forget you're a saver. Some savior you were."

"I didn't *want* to kill it!"

I thought we were on our way to another fight until I realized that last sentence had been punctuated by a sob. I walked over and turned Alex's face up and was so startled to see tears streaming down both cheeks that I didn't know what to say. I mean we're talking Alex McKinley crying here.

It took some time to get the whole story but it seemed that after I left Alex got the flashlight and finally located the intruder in the far back corner of the fireplace. It wasn't a big huge rat after all but a medium sized field mouse. So Alex got the jar and spent the better part of the hour trying to get the mouse to go in it so it could be set free. The mouse went everywhere but the jar and got more and more agitated and aggressive as time went on. Frustrated, Alex put down the poker and tried to guide it into the jar by hand. The mouse turned and attacked, biting through a work glove and piercing the skin. When Alex jumped back the mouse escaped the fireplace and ran across the room to a corner. At that point there seemed to be nothing left to do but to shoot it.

Killing that mouse was such a big deal that tears started rolling several times while telling me what happened. Alex put the mouse in some newspaper and left. It wasn't until later as I went to get the mail that I noticed a freshly turned mound of dirt in the front flowerbed.

You can tell that I've been around Alex for years now because I'm about to use a cartoon analogy, but that day I think my heart did the same thing towards Alex that the Grinch's did toward the little Whosits in Whoville on Christmas day.

I built the fire I'd been wanting. But I didn't watch the stack of videos that I'd planned on. I didn't eat the junk food I'd bought. I'm not sure I remembered to eat at all. I sat on the floor. Between the jar and the gun. And I thought about my tenderhearted housemate for the rest of the weekend.

Talk about the most complexly simple or simply complex person I have ever met. Up until that week I'd thought of Alex in very simple terms. I thought only of what Alex did to me. Not who Alex was. What I came to realize was that nothing was done *to* me. What occurred was that I *felt* more intensely when I was with Alex than I ever had before. More often than not it was anger or a feeling of transparency. But that made sense all of a sudden. The easiest emotion to have, for someone not accustomed to having any at all, is anger. And the anger was a result of having my belief systems challenged. It wasn't really anger at Alex. It was anger at myself when I realized that I'd bought into whole lines of thought, whole ways of being, without ever asking why.

When I would make a statement that sounded like status quo rhetoric Alex would bleat at me like a sheep. Literally 'baa, baa, baa'. Or point out something about me that I didn't want to know and didn't want anyone else to see, either. God, that would infuriate me. I would storm off and stay shut away for days sometimes. It never occurred to me that when I came out Alex was right there, always. Patient. Understanding. Interested in what I thought regardless of whether I'd changed my mind or stood my ground. It wasn't whether I believed as Alex did. It was whether I'd come to my own conclusion rather than blindly following someone else's.

But until the 'day the rat died' I had only been allowed to witness the irreverent, anti-establishment, question everything side. I'd recently seen Alex's compassion on the job, which seemed boundless but very, very stoic. God, if anyone should be cried over it ought to be some of the kids at that Center not some stupid rat. Getting to know Alex, I discovered, was like peeling an onion. It happened one layer at a time and it was more than likely that one or both of us was going to cry a lot before it was all over.

31

The crying started much sooner than I would have liked. I was in court all day that following Monday and was worried about making it in time for an interview at the Teen Center. I ran into the ladies room to brush my teeth, fix my hair and freshen up my makeup. I intended to meet Alex at the Center at five thirty and I was going to be cutting it close. As I ran down the main hall of the courthouse I noticed a large group of people, mostly court personnel, spilling out of the breakroom. I slowed down long enough to ask one of the clerks of court what was going on. She took her eyes off the little TV on top of a filing cabinet long enough to gasp that there had been a shooting outside of City Hall and that the whole area including the courthouse had been cordoned off.

I was going to be late and there was nothing I could do about it so I went down the hall to my office, plopped down at my desk and flipped on the television to watch another one of Chicago's dramas unfold.

The stations weren't just running breaking news updates but were all live at the scene. I thought that was odd, then it dawned on me that they had been nearby to do the story on the Teen Center's mural and must have rushed there as soon as it came over the scanner. Not surprising. Television in Chicago was notorious for opting for blood and gore over anything uplifting. So I relaxed and put my feet on the desk since I wasn't going to be late for anything. There was no way they'd have another crew at the Center. I picked up the phone to let Alex know I was safe and sound inside the courthouse and to confirm that we wouldn't be doing the interview that night.

The phone rang forever before it was picked up. There was so much background noise I couldn't tell who I was speaking to but the voice sounded familiar. I realized I was hearing the same TV broadcast in stereo through the earpiece of the phone. After asking to speak to Alex several times and getting no response I raised my voice and demanded to know who was on the other end of the line. He yelled back that it was Antoine. I yelled who I was and asked what was going on. At the same time, I swiveled my chair towards the TV. I vaguely heard Antoine yell, "Ms. Scafidi, don't you know…" as the phone hit the floor.

There was a message scrolling across the bottom of the screen saying 'taped earlier this afternoon at Chicago City Hall'. The video behind it was bouncing all over the place like it does when the cameraman is running. There was a flurry of activity around the edge of the picture. In the center and getting closer every second was a recurring nightmare that I will have for the rest of my life. It was ten maybe fifteen seconds of tape but it replays in my mind far too often for my comfort.

Alex was sitting propped against the wall that the mural had been on. Covered…I'm sorry, this is still hard for me. Covered in blood. Face, arms, chest. The wall behind had a large bloodstain and a smear running all the way down where someone had hit it and then slid to the sidewalk. I turned up the volume in time to hear '…scene of a brutal gang related slaying…' My mind wouldn't accept that it might have been Alex, who appeared very much alive at the time but was cradling and rocking a very lifeless looking body. The scene panned a few feet away in time to catch a sheet being draped over another body. I could hear Alex's voice in the background screaming, "Get the fuck away! Don't touch him!" I was halfway down the courthouse steps before I realized I'd left my chair.

It took only a minute to run the few short blocks but the scene was so dramatically different when I got there that I felt like I had time traveled. I was disoriented until I remembered that what I had seen on TV had been a rerunning of live footage taped forty five minutes to an hour previously. There was a morgue wagon at the curb and whoever had been under the sheet was no longer on the sidewalk. Paramedics had gotten Alex up and standing with assistance. Whoever had been in Alex's arms was being zipped into a body bag. I had to know who it was so I headed in that direction. I was too late. The zipper was pulled shut before I got close enough to see. But my question was answered when I heard Alex behind me.

"No! Carlos! No, no, no, no…NO!!"

My brother Tony coined a phrase when he was four to describe what my youngest brother Nick would do when he was scared and upset. He would come to me saying, 'Rissa, Rissa make Nicky stop scrying'. It was meant as a combination of screaming and crying and that was what Alex was doing. It sounded like a wild wolf in agonizing pain.

I was in complete shock and the edge of grief and disbelief over Carlos was starting to close in. I turned around and felt my heart shatter. The paramedics had gotten Alex's shirt open and were trying their best to tend to a huge gash where a bullet had plowed across the top of the right shoulder.

Alex yelled, "Get the fuck away from me!" and I saw one of the paramedics go down from a solid left hook to the jaw. He stumbled to his feet and they both backed slowly away. I heard the other one saying, '…still refusing medical treatment', into the microphone pinned to his shirtfront. The speaker squawked back and they both knelt and started packing up their kits.

It was the first clear line of sight either one of us had. There were people all over the place but we managed to push our way through until we could throw our arms around each other. We sank to our knees still holding on and stayed that way for what seemed an eternity. I was furious the next morning to find that personal moment of grief plastered all over the front page of the paper.

Kneeling there, clutching each other was the strangest experience I'd ever had. It was as though two different scenarios were playing out at the same time. On the outside I was terrified and relieved. I was trying to be as nurturing and comforting as I could be while also dealing with my own sadness. I felt confused and muddled and everything was happening too fast to absorb. I wanted to be whatever Alex needed me to be but I wasn't sure what that was.

On the inside everything was moving in slow motion and all my feelings and thoughts seemed clear and vivid. As we held each other I could feel Alex's blood soaking my blouse and spreading across my chest and I had a clear sense that we had momentarily become one. I had an actual physical sensation of it happening. In a way it all felt familiar and some part of me just let go. I saw and felt myself nestle deeper into those arms and I knew nothing could ever hurt me. I was safe and protected and I belonged there. I was acutely aware of our bodies pressing together. It was the feeling of being reunited after a long absence. I was able to put those words to it once Alex and I got together but at the time I passed it all off to traumatic hallucination.

Back in 'real time' I could feel Alex's racking sobs shaking my body. They died down and eventually stopped altogether. I felt Alex take a very deep breath and slowly let it out. It was then that I realized I was no longer holding someone destroyed by grief. Instead, I had my arms around a rigid and determined body. When I looked up there was nothing left in those hollow eyes but anger.

Alex let go of me, pried my hands away and stood up. A cop came over, and being unusually sensitive, offered condolences. He said to be at the precinct in the morning. Alex nodded, looked at me and started up the sidewalk saying, "Go home".

"What?! And where are *you* going?"

"I've got something to do."

"Alex! Are you crazy? You're hurt. You need to go to the hospital." I struggled to keep up.

"I'll go later. It doesn't hurt."

"It's a bullet wound for God's sake. You're in shock." We reached the Jeep.

Alex got in, slammed the door and unzipped the window. "No shit. Now go home. I'll be there when I get done."

"But I don't want to be alone. And I don't think you should be either."

"I won't be. And I *am* sorry you will be. But I've got to do this."

As the Jeep screeched away from the curb I yelled, "You're going to do something stupid, aren't you?"

I stood there for a long time then turned and walked back to my office for my purse and jacket. I hadn't even noticed the cold until Alex drove off and then I began to shiver uncontrollably. I got in my car to go home but found myself headed to the Teen Center instead.

Alex's Jeep was parked half on and half off the curb and there were droplets of blood leading down the sidewalk and through the front door. I went in unsure of what I would find. The street had been deserted and the Center seemed to be, too, until I heard loud voices coming from the gym. I eased up to the propped open door in time to hear Alex yell for everyone to be quiet and sit down. A hush immediately fell over the room and I listened while Alex made a dramatic and heart wrenching speech demanding that, in honor of Carlos' peaceful and gentle soul, there be no retaliation and no more bloodshed; that their families could not afford to lose any of them in an all out war; that if they had to channel their energies somewhere it should be in clear-coating Carlos' mural on the Teen Center so that no one could deface it; and if they didn't help with that then they needed to go home and be with their families who were probably worried sick about them.

I didn't understand the part about the mural but I felt better knowing this was what Alex had had to do. I was afraid I might be considered an outsider even though I'd been around the week before and I was so emotionally exhausted I was about to collapse. Feeling sure Alex would be home soon and that we would be able to grieve together, I left unnoticed.

I was alone with my sadness and worry until the following evening. Over the course of those twenty four hours I had watched the news, read the paper, called the Center at least a hundred times, called all the hospitals, called the precinct and in between it all cried myself literally sick three or four times. I had bonded with Carlos and had come to care a great deal about him in a very short period of time. But I knew my violent reaction to all this was not only about him.

I had this sickening feeling that I was on the verge of losing the Alex I was beginning to love. Yes, I said love. Although it would be almost a year after that before I openly acknowledged it and acted on it, I knew that day that I must be falling in love. I was having feelings, thoughts and fears the extent of which had no other explanation.

I don't mean lose as in physically. Not a physical death. But I could feel that there was a battle being waged somewhere for Alex's heart and soul and that was precisely what I was falling in love with. I wasn't in physical love, that would come much later. I was in emotional love, the depth of which I still have trouble fathoming.

I know all this sounds crazy. I can't explain how I knew these things. They didn't exactly come in pictures or words inside my head. It was just a 'knowing' like I'd never had before.

I knew, for instance, that all I could do was wait. That Alex would come to me when it was over and not before. I had no idea what 'it' was and I knew I probably never would. But I'd know the outcome the minute our eyes met. I would *know* who or what had won.

32

The only knowledge I had of what had happened at City Hall came from the TV and the paper. From what I understood, over the weekend a rival gang had spray painted its symbols all over the freshly whitewashed wall that Carlos had finished on Friday. The city administration, not knowing one gang from another, had assumed that it was Carlos' retaliation for having to paint over his mural. They were furious and on Monday contacted the judge in the case and insisted he issue a bench warrant. Without proof positive that Carlos did it, the judge was hesitant to have him arrested even with pressure from the Mayor. Instead, he issued an order that Carlos be located, picked up and supervised by an officer while he whitewashed the latest defacing.

The cops found him at the Center midafternoon Monday. Assuming that one of his gang brothers did it as a gesture to him, Carlos didn't argue and went with them. When they got to City Hall he was horrified to see Vice Lord insignia in red and black all over the wall. He tried to explain to the cops that he couldn't cover it up. It's supposedly the highest insult and a precursor to a gang war for one gang to deface the insignia of another gang. The cops informed Carlos that he either complied with the judge's order or they'd take him in. He couldn't afford another arrest. He'd gotten lucky the last time. One more and he'd be sent off. But he didn't want to start a war, either.

He talked the cops into calling Alex, who rushed over to mediate the situation. When that didn't work, they decided they had to take their chances and that it would be safer to do it with the police standing right there in hopes that the Vice Lords would know they'd had no choice.

In the end, none of it mattered. It was assumed the Vice Lords were nearby watching the whole thing. As soon as the last bit of red and black had been painted over, a car roared around the corner spraying bullets from an automatic weapon. The cops were spared only because they had just gone to their car to radio in that they were done.

Carlos had been hit sixteen times, ironically once for every year of his short life. An uninvolved passerby whose identity was being withheld until notification of the next of kin had been shot in the head and neck. Alex had been standing about ten to fifteen feet away from Carlos putting up the painting equipment. The paper referred to two bullet wounds, one to the shoulder and one to the head but I only remembered the one on the shoulder. Any closer to Carlos and Alex would have been dead, too.

My mind simply wasn't able to wrap itself around that thought for more than a few seconds at a time. Today, thinking of that possibility from over three years ago, can still make my knees buckle and my heart and mind scream inside the confines of my body. I felt the same that very day. I was experiencing the abject fear and heartwrenching pain that one would feel when faced with the possibility of the loss of a lifetime partner. My first thought was that I'd rather die than lose Alex. The fact that I felt that way was so confusing and frightening, my second thought was that I'd rather die than love Alex that much.

I had made a solemn promise to myself when I was eighteen that I would never, ever allow myself to love someone and had managed to stick to it. Like, care about, date, enjoy, be friends with. All those benign little words seemed safe enough. But love, really love? Never. People you love or who say they love you only ended up hurting you. And by eighteen I'd had enough hurt to last a lifetime.

I needed to quit thinking and feeling so I began my routine again. I called the Center, no answer; the hospitals, no Alex; the precinct, they put me on hold. I gave up and turned on the local news, same as I had twenty-four hours before when the nightmare had started unfolding. The reporter was standing on a sidewalk in front of some police station. She was saying that not more than twenty minutes before, two members of the Vice Lords gang had been thrown out of a moving car onto the steps of the downtown precinct. The two young men had their hands and feet hog-tied behind their backs and gags in their mouths. One had a four-inch gash across his cheek that would need immediate medical attention. The other seemed in fairly good shape but they both had bruises and scrapes where they had tumbled from the car. Duct taped to the chest of the larger boy was an Uzi and a ziploc baggie containing a block printed note saying 'Here's your shooter. The other one drove'. And it gave the address where the car could be located.

The scene shifted back to the studio and I was listening to an impromptu commentary on the inappropriateness of vigilantism when there was a thud at my front door. I ran to it and threw it open. Head hanging, looking like the last survivor of a slasher movie, Alex stumbled in the door and into my arms. My heart leapt and sank. So many conflicting feelings. I was trapped on an emotional roller coaster. Thrilled and grateful to be reunited, to be in each other's arms. Sad and scared at the blood, the weakness, the pain and grief, the tenseness and hollowness I could feel radiating from Alex. I needed to see those deep, dark brown eyes. I had to know *who* I was holding.

"Look at me," I pleaded.

All I felt was a shake of the head and a more insistent burrowing into my neck and a tighter squeeze around my waist. I wasn't feeling very patient or understanding at that moment. I was scared and had the strangest feeling that my future was hanging in the balance. I don't know why. For all I knew Alex could have been at Carlos' family's home the whole time but part of me knew better and that was the part that was beginning to panic. I went to grab a handful of hair and force the issue but instead I must have found the path the second bullet had taken right across the scalp.

Alex yelped and pulled back. "*Ow!* What are you doing?"

"Look at me, Alex. Please just look at me."

"OK. All right. But I was enjoying the other so much more."

The voice was tired. Exhausted. Weak. The eyes were sad. So very, very sad. But it was a feeble attempt at innuendo and humor. And it was music to my ears. There was a vague hint of that one-sided grin and a twitch of the eyebrow.

"Alex!" I fussed, trying to sound offended.

"Sorry. I'm too tired to watch what I say just now".

I felt a hand on each cheek. "I need you, Marissa. I really need you to help me through this. But I'll warn you ahead of time. I'll probably act like I don't."

I thought I was about to be kissed. And in that split second I realized that at that precise moment in time I wouldn't have resisted. I caught myself leaning into it until I realized I was misreading the signals. I pulled back before I made a fool of myself and recovered by moving into the caretaker role I'm so comfortable with. "You couldn't get rid of me if you wanted to. Now let's get you cleaned up, doctored and fed. How'd your hands get so torn up? You look like hell."

"Not surprising since I almost went there."

And that was all I ever heard about those lost hours, although I have my suspicions. Not that it mattered. I was simply grateful that the same Alex that had left for work that Monday morning seemed to have finally found a way back home.

33

"Wow. Once you get started you really get started."

"Oh, Sharon, I'm sorry. I didn't know all that was going to come pouring out from one simple little question. Did I even answer it?"

"Oh yes, you answered it, all right. And thank you for being willing to talk about the difficult and painful things. I have to tell you that, true to form, Alex spent six hours last night laying out the romantic, courtship part. Which, don't get me wrong, is equally important. I need the total picture here. But Alex has always been notorious for deeply burying the painful parts of life in hopes that they'll simply go away. You seem to be very aware of them and how deeply they affect you although you relate the story very matter of factly."

"I do? I was afraid I was being overly emotional."

"That may be something the two of you want to look at. You both are very intelligent people who are probably most comfortable intellectualizing your feelings. Alex prefers to focus on the romance and the emotions surrounding it to the exclusion of the painful times and issues; and you, today, focused on several of the emotional, painful times to the exclusion of any of the fun and romance. It's just a thought."

"Hmmm, I never really thought of that but maybe you're right. There was about a month or so after Carlos died that was horrible but mostly because Alex would hardly talk about it. Then one day, poof, everything was fine again."

"Consider this, some people focus on the positive aspects of life because they are so afraid of the negative consuming them. Others focus on the negative aspects because they're afraid they don't deserve the positive. That's an oversimplification but it all usually can be traced back to what we call 'family of origin' issues. In other words, what you experienced growing up. It's a hard pattern to break, but it *can* be broken."

"Alex either told you an awful lot about me or you're very good at what you do. I already feel transparent."

"Actually, at the risk of being immodest, it's a little of both. But what most people don't realize is that we *all* experience it to one degree or another. Balancing the two sides of ourselves is a learned behavior. It just takes awareness and constant practice."

"It sounds hard. But for some reason I feel better already. Thank you."

"So you'll be back?"

"Yes. I wasn't sure when I first got here. But yes, I'll be back tomorrow."

Alex

Part Two

34

Tuesday June 8, 1999 7:00PM

"Alex. You awake? How're you feeling?"

"Hey Sharon. OK I guess. I got to see Marissa for a few minutes this afternoon. She said she told you about Carlos."

"Yes she did. But only her version, which is missing a huge chunk that you seem to have neglected to share with her. Namely, everything you thought, felt and experienced. I thought we'd worked you through a lot of that wall building behavior years ago."

"We had. No, really. But this was something altogether different. I wanted to tell her everything but I was afraid I'd scare her to death. If not to death then at least as far away from me as she could get."

"Well then, tell *me* about those lost hours. You ought to know by now that you can't scare me off."

"I know. I've been trying to get rid of you for years."

"Very funny. So, tell me."

"I'm assuming you already know how it all happened. The graffiti, the other gang and all that. Okay. So where should I start? It's all basically a blur and there's really not much to tell. And it doesn't really have anything to do with Marissa and that *is* why we're doing this, isn't it?"

"Alex. Pay attention here. It has everything to do with Marissa. It was a pivotal point in your relationship. In case you didn't know, it's the first time she realized she was in love with you. I'm already beginning to think you're the closest thing to soul mates I've ever seen and I don't believe in that crap. I'm amazed at how the both of you are so intensely drawn to each other, yet you seem clueless as to how everything you each think, feel and experience affects the other. I've never known you to shy away from telling a story. And in the past, with a little push, you always tackled anything and everything head on in our sessions. That tells me there's a whole lot more to this than you're letting on. So take a deep breath and tell me what happened to you between the shooting and going home."

35

All right then, allow me to re-introduce you to the dark and bizarre side of Alex McKinley in case you've forgotten it exists. If you don't lock me up after this then I'm home free. First, let me ask you something. Do you think there's such a thing as *focused* blind rage? If so, that's what I had. I don't remember all the events of the shooting but I do remember the feelings. I felt relief when the last of the insignia was finally painted over. I knew we'd taken a huge risk in giving in to the cops and the judge's orders. Not that we had much choice but my critical thinking skills were marred by selfishness. All I could think of is that if we refused they'd probably send Carlos off this time and I couldn't stand the thought of not having him close by. I loved that kid like he was my own. No matter what he did, he was the bright spot of my every day. There was a connection there that I couldn't explain, kind of like with Marissa. It's not something that happens often to me but this kid just reached in and grabbed my heart the minute I laid eyes on him.

I considered the larger ramifications but dismissed them. I thought the Folks could probably humble themselves or offer some public gesture of apology to the Vice Lords the next day. Boy, was I naive, but sometimes that's all one gang was looking for, public embarrassment of the other. I should have known better. Things had been really hot between the two gangs for almost a year, but with no major bloodshed. A drive-by here, a hit and run there, each gang had picked off one or two of the weaker, less vigilant members of the other, but that was it. Sounds callous, I know, but in that environment *that's* considered minor.

I remember walking to the Jeep with the painting supplies, glad that we were done and ready to get back to the Center for our interview. It was going to be a big night for Carlos. I was so proud of him I was bursting at the seams. I turned to tell him to hurry up when I heard tires screech around the corner. I knew instantly. I *knew*.

I ran towards Carlos screaming for him to get down. I wasn't but a couple of strides away from him when his body slammed against the wall. I don't even remember hearing the gunshots. He looked down in total bewilderment, put his hand up to his chest, pulled it away and looked at the blood on it. He looked back at me, reached out with both hands, cocked his head and said, "Mac?" in a quizzical tone and died before he hit the ground.

Unfortunately, that part plays over and over in my mind in vivid slow motion detail. The rest is a blur. I don't remember being hit at all. I felt no pain from the bullets. That was so overshadowed by the emotional pain that it was nonexistent until Marissa poured alcohol on them a day later.

Now here's where it begins to get weird. The next thing I remember there was a large, dirty, callused hand slowly digging its way into my chest. As it tore my skin open and forced its way between my ribs I actually saw it, floating there, disembodied, performing its ugly deed. I couldn't do anything but watch. When I grabbed at it, there was nothing there. I felt no pain until it stopped groping, having found what it was looking for. I watched, horrified, as it yanked down and then out. It floated off about five feet away holding my still beating heart. Then it disappeared.

There aren't any words in our language to describe how I felt. I wanted to howl like a dying animal until I could taste the coppery flavor of blood in the back of my throat. According to Marissa, I did, but I don't remember.

Whatever that thing took from me, it left nothing of goodness behind. It left a black hole that desperately needed filling. The next thing I remember is seeing Marissa. If I could just get to her, I thought, she'll give me what I need. If I could just wrap my arms around her I might be able to plug that hole with something good and pure. I remember wondering if I would be able to feel my love for her without a heart.

And then she was there and I could feel the warmth coming from her. I could feel the hole beginning to close. I started to feel grief born of love for Carlos rather than grief born of rage. She squeezed harder and I felt the twinges of my love for her and I squeezed back. We sank to our knees and I started to cry. Then I felt a tap on my shoulder. I looked up and over Marissa and there was that hand, holding my heart, attached to a dark, undefined, hulking shape. It slowly and deliberately spat in my face and then disappeared.

And that was it. No more sadness, no more love, no more warmth. Hate. Nothing but cold, angry hate. I looked up in time to see the black body bag being unceremoniously thrown in the back of the coroner's wagon.

The next thing I remember after that is standing in the gym at the Center. According to everyone there, I gave a moving tribute to Carlos and a desperate and effective plea for no more violence. I suppose in the deeper recesses there was still a part of me left that truly didn't want anyone else to get hurt. But at the time, the black hole of hate was running the show and it simply didn't want a lot of people out there getting in its way.

When everyone left, I called Antoine and Tyrone into my office. "I know you two can find those shooters. Quietly, discreetly and safely. Do it."

"But you said…"

"Forget what I said in there. You want them don't you?"

"Fuck yeah we want 'em."

"Then do it. But bring them back here in one piece."

"But Mac…"

"*Do it!*"

They made their gang signs to one another, high fived and left. I sat and waited. I didn't sleep; I didn't hurt; I didn't think; I didn't move. When I felt hunger, I chewed on my hate and anger. And I waited.

No one came to the Center, not that night and not the next day. The phone started ringing off the hook that night and after a few times I calmly ripped the cord out of the wall. I heard people comment later that they had headed there that next day but as they got close they veered off and went elsewhere.

Tyrone and Antoine didn't come back until a little after noon the next day. They opened the door to my office and shoved two African American boys in ahead of them. One was no more than fifteen or sixteen, short and slightly built. The other was older, maybe late teens or early twenties and big, like he worked out a lot. They both had their hands tied behind their backs and duct tape over their mouths. Antoine forced both of them to their knees. Tyrone held up an Uzi with a bandanna wrapped around it to keep his prints off of it. He put it on my desk, "This one's your shooter," pointing at the big guy, "found this in his trunk. Other one's your driver. Think they're brothers but they ain't talkin'. Little one was packing this in his pants." He laid down a nine-millimeter semiautomatic handgun.

I dropped my feet off the desk and stood up. Went to the cabinet, got latex gloves out of the first aid kit and pulled them on. I ripped the tape off of the big one on my right first, then off of the little one. They hardly flinched. The thing that infuriated me even more was that there was no fear in their eyes, just a kind of vacant defiance. I wanted to see fear before they died.

I could feel my insides building up like a pressure cooker. My eyes narrowed, my jaw clenched. I saw little sparkles of light in the room and everything took on the brownish red color of an old photograph. I reached over and casually picked up the handgun.

I leaned back against the desk and crossed my arms. "I want to know why," I said through clenched teeth.

The big one shrugged. "Cuz he dissed the brotherhood."

I got in his face and screamed, "You set him up to dis you, you son of a bitch!"

The little one snickered and said, "Like shootin' fish in a barrel."

I whirled around and backhanded him across the face with the muzzle of the gun. The sight on the end ripped him open from his cheekbone to the corner of his mouth. I could see teeth through the gash before the blood started.

The big one yelled, "Hey! Motherfucker!," and tried to stand up. I shoved the gun under his chin so hard that I helped lift him to his feet. We stood there glaring at each other, chests heaving. I leaned towards him and whispered, "I'm going to personally send you to hell where you belong."

He calmly whispered back, "I was already going, motherfucker, but I guess now I'll be seeing you there."

I started squeezing the trigger. There was a brilliant flash of light and I heard my name screamed inside my head.

36

I gotta tell you Sharon, the mind is an incredible, amazing thing. Isn't it? It's capable of processing enormous amounts of information in the blink of an eye. It always amazes me when I think of things like dreams. They say that dreams that seem to span hours happen in just minutes. Whatever happened in my office that day was like that but even faster, like no time had elapsed at all.

I saw the blinding light and heard my name. I turned to see who was screaming at me and I knew it was me even though he didn't look anything like me. He had shoulder length light brown hair, blue eyes, broad shoulders and a couple of day's growth of beard. He was wearing a natural leather tunic with fringe, some indiscriminate pants and lace up the front, knee high, leatherskin boots. He sat casually on a stump; leaning over with a big bone handled knife, carving something that looked like it might end up being a flute.

He glanced up at me, went back to carving and said, "Alex, what're you doing?"

I was so completely taken off guard that all I could muster was a feeble, "Huh?"

He sighed as though he thought I was more trouble than I was worth. He got up and walked over to me and thumped me on the chest with the tip of his knife in rhythm to his words. "I would suggest that before you pull that trigger, you know for sure exactly who and what you really want to kill."

And then he was gone. I was back in the office still squeezing the trigger when his words hit home. I had committed to pulling it. I knew I couldn't stop it from happening. I heard myself scream, *"NO!"* jerked my arm away and blew a hole in the filing cabinet.

I threw the gun across the room so hard that the cheap grip on the handle shattered. I turned and shoved the boy I almost shot, as hard as I could, towards Antoine and yelled for he and Tyrone to get them out of there. All four of them looked more frightened then than at any other time. I must have looked like a lunatic. I certainly felt like one. They scrambled to get out of the office.

The rage was not gone but it was suddenly turned inward. I didn't want to kill that boy. I remembered only three days before having to kill a tiny field mouse and how my heart had felt like it was breaking. Had I killed that boy I knew my soul would have shattered into a million pieces.

What I wanted to kill was the part of me that felt responsible for Carlos' death. Those boys were nothing more than victims of the rules, regulations and beliefs of the system they had chosen to be a part of. The same thing that had led them to kill without conscience had led me to put someone I cherished in a situation that cost him his life. I had buckled to the rules, the expectations of the system. We're not to believe in a higher truth. A higher, more universal right. Don't question judges. Don't argue with cops. Just do as you're told. Live inside the box we've created for you. Don't color outside the lines.

I saw his face again, right before he died. I heard him say, "Mac?" in that questioning tone. It haunts me to this day that he might not have been trying to say, "Mac? What happened?" but instead, "Mac? Why'd you let this happen?"

I felt sick and vomited into the trashcan. I yelled his name at the top of my lungs and swept everything off the top of my desk. At that point everything went black. I have no clue how long I was gone but excruciating pain in my hands brought me back.

I was standing with my forehead against the tall double-door metal cabinet. My face was swollen from crying and my cheeks and shirtfront were soaked with tears and sweat combined with the blood from my shoulder and head. I realized I was punching the doors with one fist and then the other. Right hand, "I'm sorry"; left hand, "Forgive me."

I must have been doing it for a while and with vengeance. Both doors were buckled inward and looked like they'd been beaten with a golf club. There was fresh blood on both doors and as I turned and slid to the floor I noticed my hands looked and felt like raw meat with little bits of latex glove left here and there. I realized I wasn't alone anymore and looked up to see Tyrone squatting in front of me.

"Carlos loved you, Mac. He'd never blame you. But those two in there have got to go down for this."

"No more killing, Ty. It's got to stop." He nodded, reached under my arms, lifted me up on my feet and hugged me. And with that I think I got my first little piece of heart back.

We decided to deliver them to the cops. We knew they'd be hard on them for several reasons. One being that it was only sheer luck that two of their own weren't killed as well. Two, that the community was blaming the City for the two deaths rather than the Vice Lords and the administration needed to wrap this up with swift and strict consequences. And thirdly, there were enough Folks members in the county prison to make their stay there very, very unpleasant.

So we gagged and hog-tied them, packaged the evidence, threw them in the back of the Jeep and dumped them at a side entrance to the local precinct. There was a black cop standing outside smoking a cigarette when we did it. He simply nodded at us and went back inside.

I dropped Tyrone and Antoine on the corner near where they lived and headed home. Hoping Marissa was all right and knowing I could never tell her how close I'd come to losing it all.

37

"So you're telling me that you're still seeing things and hearing voices after all these years?"

"God damn it, Sharon! That's all you got out of that?"

"No Alex. That's not all I got. But I am a psychologist. I'm supposed to pick up on minor things like that, you know. You can't wave red flags at me and expect me to not notice."

"For your information, I've done a lot of research since I was last on your couch and there are other explanations for it besides being crazy."

"I've never said, nor have I ever thought, you were crazy, Alex. But for such a highly functional, logical, analytical person you've got to admit you have experiences that fall outside of the norm to say the least."

"Okay. I'll grant you that much. But it's happened off and on my whole life. You reach a certain level of acceptance after a while, even if you don't understand it. There's always a message and if nothing else I've learned to pay attention."

"Well at least they don't turn evil and instruct you to do immoral or dangerous acts. That's when I'd start to worry."

"Oh, I see and hear evil occasionally, now. But it's always an adversary never an ally."

"Do me a favor and don't tell anyone else that. They'll take my license for not referring you for heavy medication."

"That's very validating, Sharon. You're quite the comedian today. Now can I get back to the story at hand?"

"By all means, go ahead."

38

Pulling in that driveway was like finding an oasis in a desert. The only thing that got me from the Jeep to the front door was the memory of what it had felt like to be held by her, kneeling on the sidewalk twenty-four hours earlier. I needed that again. I may have resisted the temptation of hate but I still had an emotional hole in my chest and I knew she was the only one who could help me fill it.

It took the better part of a month before I began to feel whole again. Without Marissa I probably would have crawled inside a bottle and never come out. Up to that point I had carried the friendship pretty much on my own. Not that she hadn't participated but I'd taken most of the initiative. Something kicked in for her when Carlos died. I guess now I know it was love. But I didn't know exactly what it was then. She took over. We'd have never made it if she hadn't.

I wanted to withdraw from the whole world. Just crawl into a hole and pull a rock across the opening but she wouldn't let me.

I don't know how she did it day in and day out. She was everything I needed exactly when I needed it. I was sarcastic, angry, tearful, rejecting, needy, difficult, unresponsive, clingy, depressed, manic. You name it. From one extreme to another. Completely unpredictable. She rode the waves with patience and understanding. She didn't put up with any crap but she never wavered.

She instinctively knew when to push and when not to; when to come around and when to stay away; when to make me talk and when to just sit quietly beside me for hours. That first week she doctored my wounds, made me eat, made me sleep, shielded me from reporters and took the bottle away from me when she thought I'd had enough. When I'd lash out and tell her to mind her own business she'd calmly tell me that for the time being I *was* her business.

For the first time in my life I felt understood and accepted. And those are the two things that can make me feel more loved than any thing or any words. I wanted to give that back. I wanted her to feel loved. I wanted to help her through this like she was helping me. But I had nothing inside to give. I was like a sponge that needed to soak it all up before I could give anything back.

She went with me to the funeral that following Saturday and held my hand throughout the church service and at the graveside. There were TV cameras at the cemetery but she held on anyway. The ABC affiliate had made a big deal over the fact that they'd had an exclusive interview scheduled with Carlos the very night he was murdered and they had been playing it to the hilt all week.

Some other time I would have been more sensitive to what she might hear from her family or friends but I felt as if her touch was all that was holding me together. Carlos' mother came up to us after the service holding a wrapped box. "I don't know what's in it but he had me wrap it up that mornin'. Said it was for the both of you." Her composure collapsed and she started sobbing uncontrollably. Between gasps she managed to choke out the words, "He respected you. When he didn't respect nobody else, he respected you. I got to honor that." She extended the box in my direction.

I took it gently from her hands. It seemed to be a shoebox, covered in metallic purple paper and tied the width and length of it with thin yellow ribbon. I just stared at it. My hands started trembling and got progressively more violent until you could hear the contents thumping inside the box. Marissa put her hands on mine to still them but that just made it worse. She finally took the box from me and I shoved my hands in my pockets and stared at the ground.

Marissa handled it with complete grace. "Ms. Diaz, we're both so sorry for your loss. Alex and I cared a great deal about Carlos. That's why I hope you understand that opening this gift needs to be a very private moment for both of us."

Ms. Diaz looked disappointed but nodded her agreement. She and Marissa hugged briefly. She turned to me and stroked my cheek while tears quietly streamed down both our faces. I knew she was telling me that she loved me for loving her son. Then she turned and walked slowly back to the fresh grave, crossed herself and sank to her knees. Marissa put a hand on my elbow and guided me to the car.

We drove home in silence with the box sitting between us. We took it into the house and set it on my coffee table. I went to the kitchen to pour myself a drink. I was standing at the counter when Marissa came in. She wrapped her arms around me from behind and laid her head against my back. There were so many times over the course of that month where if I'd had any capacity for it, things could have quickly turned sexual. That was one of those times. But it just wasn't there. My guess is that she sensed that and felt safe being so physical or maybe that's where she wanted it to go but I just couldn't get there. I don't know. We've never talked about it.

She reached out until she found the bottle and pushed it across the counter out of my reach. She squeezed me and said, "Alex, three's a crowd. Let's leave Jack Daniels out of this and go open that box. Just the two of us. Let's get it over with so we can deal with it."

I turned around to face her, pulled her to me and rested my chin on the top of her head. We stayed like that for a little while until I pulled back and kissed her chastely on the forehead. She stepped back and held out her hand. I took it and we went into the living room and sat on the couch.

My hands were shaking too much to untie the ribbon so I held the box in my lap while Marissa opened it. First the ribbon, then the paper, then the box top.

On top of something wrapped in tissue paper was a hand written note on spiral notebook paper with the fringe still attached to the side. It was in the labored printing of a child trapped in a young man's body.

HEY MAC,

> TONITES THE BIG NITE. MY BIG
> PREMEER. HA! THOT YOU MITE
> WANT THIS BACK SEEIN AS HOW
> I WONT BE NEEDIN IT ENYMORE.
> IM GONA TAKE SCAFITI UP ON HER
> OFER AN DO REAL ART WITH HER.
> YOU KNOW BRUSHS AN SHIT. SHE
> TURND OUT TO BE ALRITE. YOU
> BETER TREET HER RITE. SEE YOU
> TONITE. THANKS FOR BELEEVIN.

> CARLOS
> (VAN GO)

It was a damn good thing it was written in pencil or it would have been ruined by my tears. I finished it and handed it to Marissa who only got about halfway through before she let out a soft moan and put her head in her hands saying, "I can't. I can't read this."

I reached in the box and pulled out the lump of tissue paper. Inside it was an old, dark brown, cracked leather glove. The first two fingers of it were stiff and covered in layers of paint. The rest of the glove was spotted all over with every color imaginable. The last time he'd worn it was working with Marissa on the mural.

I held it to my cheek and realized it smelled like him. I broke down after that and it took some time before I could explain the history of it to Marissa.

About two or so years before when I was first getting to know Carlos he kept coming to the Center with paint all over his right hand. Half the time it was still tacky and he would leave multicolored fingerprints all over everything. I called him in my office one day and asked him what the deal was. He told me about how you couldn't help but get it on your hands when you used spray paint. I read him the riot act and told him I didn't approve of graffiti and for him not to come back unless he cleaned up his act, literally and figuratively. He claimed it wasn't graffiti and begged me to come and see it. He guided me all over the neighborhood after work that day. I was shocked to see that he was covering up old graffiti with really impressive pictures. Big, little, simple, elaborate. It was amazing. I admitted the error of my accusations and took him to a hardware store and bought him a nice pair of leather work gloves to keep his hands clean.

Marissa took the glove from me, wrapped it back up and put it and the note back in the box. She pulled me to her and we lay on the couch together, my head on her chest, her fingers stroking my hair. All she could say was, "I can't believe he's gone," over and over. We cried ourselves to sleep like that.

39

I took two more weeks off from work and by the end of the second one I was becoming moderately functional again. I was making myself get up, workout, eat three meals a day, shower and put on clean clothes. It was an effort but I made myself go through the motions. I was actually proud of myself for having managed two days in a row.

Marissa had to go back to work the second week but she called regularly to check up on me. I tried laying off the heavy drinking because I knew it scared her. It was a painfully slow process but I recognized that I'd taken a few baby steps towards healing.

Marissa had been gently pushing me to go back to work. I didn't know if I could ever set foot back in that office and I couldn't tell her all the reasons why. That dilemma was quickly solved when the President of the Board showed up on my doorstep the Friday before I was due back, to regretfully, I love that word, don't you? Regretfully ask for my resignation. He must have been confident that he'd get it because he'd taken the liberty of packing up all my stuff and putting the boxes on the porch. He cited the list of my transgressions to drive the point home. I didn't have it in me to remind him that I'd been considered wonderful for the four years prior to the twenty-four hour time period in question. Or the fact that I'd been shot twice and watched two people murdered right in front of me.

Instead, I just looked him in the eye and told him I didn't give a fuck what any of them thought and I slammed the door in his face.

I really went downhill from there. I don't know which was worse, the hell I lived in the rest of that month or the hell I put Marissa through. I'm not sure what happened but my depression broke like a fever around the first of May. I just woke up one day and thought, 'I can't do this anymore'. I knew that if I was waiting for the pain and sadness over Carlos to go away before I began to live again that I'd be waiting till the end of time. You can only hide and lick your wounds for so long before you get a hairball.

It was a Wednesday and Marissa had already left for work probably assuming I'd sleep until noon as usual. She'd been my life support for that month. I do believe she was the only thing that kept me mentally, emotionally and spiritually alive. Come to think of it, probably physically, too. But there's a huge difference between alive and living. Living is an action word and I was ready to do it again.

I hadn't meditated in a long, long time but I felt compelled to that morning. People think meditation is some weird hocus pocus mumbo jumbo. You may be one of them for all I know. But put very simply, for me, it's mastering the ability to be completely still and quiet your mind so that what needs to come can come. I don't cross my legs; I don't stare at a candle; I don't say OM.

I propped up in the bed, worked on my breathing and cleared my mind. Then I simply asked for some guidance. A few moments passed as I worked on staying relaxed and open. Then there was a flash of light behind my eyelids and I was standing in a beautiful forest glen. I turned slowly around, taking it all in until I noticed the same leather clad fellow sitting on the same stump carving what appeared to be the same flute.

He motioned for me to come over and I started walking towards him.

"Come on Alex, we haven't got all day. It doesn't work that way."

"Where am I? Who *are* you?"

"You're here and I'm you."

"I figured that much out last time. Are you me past or future?"

"Time is irrelevant to the issue at hand."

"Is that the same flute as a month ago?"

"You're really new at this aren't you?"

"Well, yeah."

"You'll have to figure out the finer points on your own time. Now, you asked for some guidance. It's about time you snapped out of it. I realize you live in an era that promotes self pity but God Almighty, you were downright pathetic."

"Hey!"

"Be quiet and listen. Carlos had other things to do somewhere else. He would have died somehow, somewhere at that precise moment regardless of whether or not you even existed. The way it happened, he gave you the gift of facing your personal demons and overcoming them. You also came face to face with your own mortality so you should be more appreciative of what you've got. You've got a wonderful woman in your life who cares very deeply about you and you've worried her sick. You've been released from the bonds of your previous employment so you can follow a new path. Quit feeling like everyone's abandoned you. You're the one who's abandoned you. Go home and learn to be grateful."

I was stunned. It would have made me mad except I knew it was all true. Especially the part about feeling abandoned. I wasn't sure what to say.

"Well, uh…thank you…uh, what do I call you? I can't call you me, that's too confusing."

"You can call me Ethan. But don't call me often. You've got to do some of this on your own."

There was another flash and I was back in my room. I wasn't sure if that was the most incredible experience of my life or if the little men in white coats needed to come get me with their butterfly nets. It always seems so right and so normal when it's happening but when it's over you can't help but wonder if you're looney tunes. My mind was doubting as always but deep down in my heart I knew it was real.

I felt refreshed and inspired. I took a deep breath, jumped up and got busy. I cleaned the house from top to bottom and started on laundry. I raised the blinds and threw open the windows to let in the spring day. I cleaned out the refrigerator and cabinets of all my depression food and poured an almost full fifth of whiskey down the drain.

I went to the grocery store and stocked up on healthy food and specialty items. I bought four flats of flowers for the flowerbeds and a dozen each of pink and yellow roses for Marissa. I figured red ones might be a little much. I got home, planted the flowers, showered and started an elaborate meal. Right before time for her to get home I ran her a hot bubble bath, in my tub since I promised to stay out of her bathroom, lit candles and put them around the tub and floated rose petals from half the roses on top of the bubbles. I propped a thank you card on the soap dish.

I heard her car in the driveway and I snuck a peek at her through the front window. She got out of the car, walked up the sidewalk, stared at the flowerbed on the right then the one on the left and back at the one on the right. She looked up the street, down the street and then turned around and looked across the street. I gathered she was looking for clues to the flower fairy's identity.

She shrugged and came up on the porch, got her mail and unlocked her door. I heard her briefcase drop on the floor as usual. She came through the connecting door with her head down, sifting through her mail. She absently called out, "Alex, did you know somebody planted…". She came to an abrupt stop and her voice trailed off. I was leaning against the archway between the living room and dining room. I watched her nose twitch as she smelled the combination of lemon scented furniture polish and dinner. Quite different from the stale, depressing, whiskey scented air of the last month, I was sure. She looked up and saw the nicely set table and let the mail fall from her hands. Her head whipped around and she spotted me, clean, dressed and vertical for a change.

I said, "Welcome home."

She rushed the few steps towards me and threw herself at me. I caught her in mid air and swung her around.

"Oh God, Alex, you're back. You've come back. You're back. You're back. You're back."

She was choking me and I had to set her down and pry her arms from around my neck so I could breathe. She grabbed my face and said, "Let me look at you. Oh my God, you're back," She stared into my eyes. "You're in there, you're really in there."

I felt like a soldier, home from a war I wasn't expected to survive.

I poured her a glass of wine and led her back to the bathroom. She was on the verge of tears when she saw the roses on the vanity, the candles, the bubble bath. There were fresh towels laid out and one of my big terry cloth robes. When she turned to me I saw the question in her eyes, wondering if I was planning on joining her. She looked a little apprehensive, but I got the sense that with a little finesse I probably could have. But this wasn't about that. I told her to relax, enjoy herself and that dinner would be ready in forty-five minutes.

She came padding down the hall right on time. We didn't talk much during dinner. There wasn't much to say. But we took our time and enjoyed ourselves. At one point she reached over and held my free hand.

"I missed you Alex. I really, really missed you."

"Yeah, I missed me, too."

We finished dinner around seven thirty and she'd been stifling yawns for thirty minutes. Before she could say anything I told her, "You're full, you're relaxed and you're exhausted from a month of playing nursemaid to an emotional invalid. Go to bed. I promise I'll still be here in the morning." I walked her to the door.

She reached up and patted my cheek. "You promise?"

"Cross my heart."

She started walking away, paused for a few seconds and then turned around.

"I know I shouldn't ask, but what happened? What brought you back?"

"Let's just say I gave myself a good talking to and leave it at that."

40

Marissa's birthday was that Sunday, the fifth of May. She turned thirty-six. Her family was having a dinner for her on Friday with aunts and uncles and cousins. She invited me but understood when I declined. If they had started their prejudiced banter, and they inevitably would, we both knew I wouldn't keep my mouth shut. Not to mention the fact that they didn't seem to like me one bit. Seems I had corrupted their daughter. If they only knew the ways I wanted to corrupt her, they'd have had a collective stroke.

Marissa tried to pump herself up all week to be brave enough to confront their prejudices when it started. But we both knew she was walking into a damned if you do, damned if you don't situation. I didn't want her setting herself up for failure. By simply no longer participating herself, she'd be sending a clear enough message for the first go round.

I waited up for her that night and she came in awfully sullen for a birthday girl. She didn't want to rehash the entire evening but did go so far as to say that she stood her ground. Her brother Tony had been the worse and even resorted to name-calling. She said she stayed quiet but steadfast until he began attacking me as the source of her new opinions. She blew up at him for the first time in her life and really let him have it. Which, of course, just seemed to confirm his opinion that I had been playing mind games with her and who knew what other kinds of games.

That really made her angry and defensive which he in turn thought answered his implied question to the affirmative. It ended when he said he'd 'go beat my fucking brains out' and Marissa walked out on her own party.

I was proud of her but she felt miserable and guilty. It was not only her first time to rock the boat with her family but to the best of her knowledge the first time any female in the family had caused a commotion. The men argued, fought, yelled and screamed all the time. But the women were expected to stay on the sidelines and unquestionably support the side of whichever male was closest to them in blood or marriage.

It felt good that she came to my defense but I felt guilty because I knew I *was* the cause of the change in Marissa. I hadn't fed her any of her new thoughts but I had offered her an environment where she had the freedom to have them. Since I usually teased her about her emotional narcolepsy, she made a joke about it and said she thought she'd turn in early so she could sleep it off before morning.

The next day was our day to celebrate. I took her on a day long outing in the country. We took the top off the Jeep, went to a quiet, little known place on the lake, picnicked and stopped at every antique shop and junk shop on the way back. There was an old bronze lamp with a stained glass shade that she fell in love with at one place. I had the shop owner box it up and sneak it into the Jeep while I distracted her.

It was a wonderful day and we were both pleasantly exhausted by the time we made it back home. We said goodnight and I heard her get in her shower. I raced to the Jeep, got the package and ignoring our rules, managed to get it onto her bedside table and plugged in before she got out of the shower.

I hurried back to my side turning off lights as I went, got undressed and jumped in bed and pretended to be sound asleep. I tend to forget how long she can piddle around in the bathroom before, during and after a shower so I must have actually fallen asleep.

She scared the life out of me when she launched herself onto my bed forcefully enough to bounce me completely up off it. I woke up in mid air. She bounced me around a couple more times for good measure and then plopped cross-legged at the end of the bed facing me. There was just enough light filtering into the room to see that her hair was wet and she was wearing my robe that she'd never given back.

"Oh, Alex it's wonderful. Thank you."

"You're welcome. Sorry about going in your room."

"Oh that. I'm beginning to think those rules might be a little extreme. Besides, I want to see what your room looks like. Can I turn on the light?"

"Sure, go ahead." It was the only room that I'd put any work into and I wanted her to see it, too.

"This is really nice."

"Thanks. I intended to start in here and move up through the rest of the house but haven't gotten any further."

I had painted that room when I first moved in. The walls were a rich red brick. The baseboards, ceiling molding and windows were a French vanilla. It had an old refinished four poster bed I'd inherited, an armoire, dresser, bookshelf and bedside tables. None of which matched but all of which were antique and complimented each other nicely. Under the bed and taking up most of the room was an old Persian rug. There was a rocking chair in one corner with an ornate torchere floor-lamp beside it. A little crowded but obviously my inner sanctum. I think she was rather surprised.

After she'd taken it all in she got up and turned the light back off. She looked up at the ceiling and gasped. I had hundreds of little glow in the dark stars pasted over the entire ceiling. It looked like the Milky Way. She found her way around the bed and lay down on the other side, mesmerized. She was quiet for awhile as we both lay there staring at the ceiling.

"Could you do this for me in my room?"

I rolled over under the covers and propped up on one elbow and suddenly realized I didn't have a stitch of clothes on and was lying there in bed with her. I could feel myself start to hyperventilate. I croaked out a "Sure."

"That would be so neat. It would be like that song from that movie. What was it? 'Somewhere Out There' or something like that. I could be looking at my stars and know you were looking at yours at the same time." She rolled over to face me and started to reach out for me like it was something she'd done a thousand times. When she realized what she was doing she practically levitated off the bed, stammered something about it being late and was gone down the hall.

41

The whole summer went about like that. I don't mean to say she spent the summer running away from me although she did her share of that. Or maybe it would be more appropriate to call it running from herself. What I mean is that the rest of the summer had no major events or crises but was a very steady growing together. We became more and more inseparable which in retrospect may or may not have been a good thing. It's my natural state to be a virtual loner and I'm very comfortable with it. Marissa's naturally a social and family creature and she couldn't seem to merge the two. Her family and friends thought I was simply too far afield from the Marissa they knew and they could see her changing from our association. The more they all tried to convince her to stay away from me, the less time she spent with them.

What they didn't seem to understand was that the changes in Marissa didn't have anything to do with whether or not she was drawn to me or attracted to me. It had to do with her coming into her own. This was a personal growth period that she had been standing on the edge of for years but no one had been there to support her taking that first big step. They'd all been actively holding her back, actually, because they were comfortable with the Marissa they had created and they wanted her to stay that way.

It was an incredible process to watch. That night that she told me about her childhood had pried the door open. She stood in that doorway for a short while but once she stepped through she never looked back. She gobbled up new experiences and new ideas like she was ravenous. The spectrum of emotions available to her broadened. She didn't always know what to do with them but preferred them over simply being either shutdown or angry. I don't know any other way to put it. She became a whole human being. She grew into herself.

And she taught me so much in return. Being an only child makes me not very good at sharing or taking turns. I had a very bad habit of just taking over and doing things my way. Once she found her voice, she didn't hesitate to tell me to back off or butt out. She helped me learn to take the edge off my know it all attitude. And she challenged *my* beliefs and opinions at every turn. I was used to people either blowing me off as being too intense or just abjectly believing whatever I said because I said it with an air of authority. We grew towards an equality I'd always said I wanted, but when faced with it, found more challenging than I thought it would be. I hadn't been challenged in a very long time and I discovered how much I liked it.

We played like children, laughed like hyenas, debated like politicians in an election year. Our trust level increased exponentially and our boundaries at home all but disappeared. We moved about in the house as if everything belonged to both of us. I taught her how to lift weights and she tried to teach me to paint. I started my own business as a grant writing and program-planning consultant. I decided after Carlos I wasn't ready for private practice yet. Marissa helped me put together the legal and tax end of working out of the house. She considered hanging out her own shingle and our even moving in together on one side and using the other side as office space but in the end she decided to stay with the City.

My thirty-first birthday rolled around while I was out of town several days in September working on a contract with a domestic violence agency in the southern part of the state. I was glad to see it come and go unnoticed. Birthdays are not good times for me, as you well know.

I got in on Saturday night around eight o'clock. Three hours later than I had expected due to traffic, rain and construction detours. Marissa's BMW was in the drive but the house was completely dark. I went in my side, dropped my bags in the living room and headed down the hall for a shower. I was hot and tired and grundgy from a frustrating day on the road and it was all I could think of. At least until I walked past the connecting door for the two sides of the house. It was closed.

I just stood there and stared at it. No matter which way I cocked my head or whether I put my hands on my hips, crossed my arms or ran both hands through my hair, it was still closed. I guess I thought if I stared at it long enough it would magically open and all would be right with the world yet again. But it didn't. And I didn't quite know what to do about that.

My neurotic and catastrophizing mind came up with a myriad of reasons. All of them bad. All of them resulting in a loss of Marissa one way or another. I couldn't figure out how this happened. I was only gone four days! I tested the door to see if it was locked from her side. It wasn't, so that ruled out half of the scenarios in my head. But there was still the problem of the other half.

My stomach was churning but I decided to get it over with. I pulled the door open and tried to sound nonchalant when I called her name. I heard suspicious sounds coming from her living room, one of which was most assuredly a giggle. And I could tell that there was definitely a male presence in the house. Had the lights been on I would have assumed one or both brothers. But with the lights off I feared the worst.

I kicked myself for having been so conservative with the expression of my feelings. I should have just laid all my cards on the table long ago and let the chips fall where they may. Now I was going to look like a fool no matter what. I decided it could go one of two ways. I could walk in there and realize my worst fear and slink back out. Or I could walk in, declare my love for her and have some kind of awful emotional showdown. I didn't like either of those choices, but I had to do something, I'd already called out to her.

I took a deep breath, threw my shoulders back and marched towards her living room like I owned the place. Only then could I see flickering candlelight. 'I knew it!', I thought to myself. But then the lights flew on and I thought, 'What am I supposed to say? Aha! Caught you doing something that you have every right to do since I've been such a tight lipped idiot?' I knew I didn't exactly have the upperhand in this.

But there wasn't time for any of that. A rehearsed and synchronized 'Surprise!' vibrated through the room followed by various forms of 'Happy Birthday'. Marissa walked up to me, grinning from ear to ear, holding a large birthday cake covered with candles.

"Make a wish," she said.

"Believe me, I already have," I said and blew out the candles.

She had pulled together quite a motley crew and I was thrilled to see them all. Antoine, Tyrone, Lavon in a brand new wheelchair, and girl-friends Latisha, Cynthia and Vanessa. About the time someone shoved a beer in my hand I noticed they all seemed a little tipsy, Marissa included. She pulled me aside and informed me that my being three hours late had made them all slightly difficult to keep amused until she had broken out the beer and wine and a couple of decks of cards.

I had seen them all here and there over the summer when I would make a point to drive through the old neighborhood. I was persona non grata at the Center per the new director so it was hard to keep in touch. The image of what Marissa must have gone through to pull that party together was as wonderful as the event itself.

However, drinking and birthdays don't mix well for me so by the time we had played spades and talked till midnight my depression was becoming evident to all. By the time our guests finally called it a night and we got the house cleaned up and put back in order it was after one in the morning. Marissa had put down the wine several hours before and was sobering up, but I had marched steadily onward.

I wanted to go to bed but she wouldn't hear of it. She used the pretense of giving me my gift but I knew she was after more than that. We sat on the couch and I opened the present. It was a beautiful watch with a rolled leather band. On the back was inscribed, A—MIZPAH—M. The word, she told me, refers to a biblical passage in the Old Testament which reads, 'May the Lord watch between me and thee, while we are absent one from another'. She jokingly said that somebody needed to keep an eye on me when she wasn't around, but I could see in her eyes that the sentiment went much deeper. It harkened back to Carlos' shooting and I knew she meant when I was emotionally absent from her as well as physically. I put it on that night and have worn it every day since, going on three years now. I read the back every morning when I put it on and every night when I take it off. And I truly believe it has protected me on more than one occasion.

But it didn't protect me that night from her probing questions. I ducked and dodged for a while but finally gave up. Never try to avoid the questions put to you by an adept attorney. It's just a waste of time. I finally caved in and told her the whole orphanage and adoption story. I won't bore you yet again with the details since you've heard it all before. It came out in a flood as usual and she sat with me for what seemed like hours. Oh, and you'll be happy to know she agreed with you about what I needed to do to bring it all to closure. Which, by the way, I finally did and at the moment regret more than words can say, thank you very much.

It did, however, feel good that night to get it off my chest. It was the one wall I'd not let down for her and I think it helped her to understand me on a much deeper level. I withdrew from her slightly after that. You know what a vulnerable revelation that is for me, but it didn't last too long.

Things got back to normal fairly quickly. We'd gotten much better during that summer of coming back into balance with each other after something would knock us askance. Although the next thing to hit us packed a one-two punch and almost knocked us out.

42

It was mid November and you could tell winter was on its way. We'd had a wonderful fall of picnics and day hikes; driving to little out of the way towns for fall festivals, even spending the night at bed and breakfast inns on several occasions. Separate beds of course but even without that one aspect I still felt like I was in a serious relationship. And the best one I'd ever had. Work was going well for both of us and Marissa had started painting in earnest again.

I got home one Saturday afternoon early, having been out of town overnight. I was hoping she and I could catch a movie and maybe dinner. I'd been putting in a lot of hours lately, trying to help several agencies prepare for their fiscal year end in December and we'd not been able to spend much time together those past few weeks.

She wasn't home so I passed the time getting the house ready for the upcoming winter weather. By the time I'd made the rounds of all the doors and windows and had weatherproofed the swing it was getting late. I hadn't paid much attention to the lack of a note when I first got home but it was beginning to weigh on my mind. I fixed dinner, watched a ballgame and when I couldn't keep my eyes open any longer, went to bed. I just assumed she was at her Mom and Pop's and knowing I shouldn't call over there, I let it go.

I woke to the sound of my name and squinted at the clock on the bedside table. It was a little past two o'clock in the morning. Marissa was standing there in an oversized T-shirt that barely came down to mid-thigh. Who says dreams don't come true?

"Alex?" Tentative.

"Mmm hmmm. Huh? What?" I struggled to completely wake up.

"Can I sleep in here tonight?" She sounded scared. Slightly needy.

"Oh. Uh…yeah, sure…I, uh…just let me get a blanket and pillow and I'll go get on the couch." I was confused but trying to be cooperative.

"Don't be dense, Alex. If I wanted to sleep alone I'd have stayed in my own bed." Exasperated, but still an edge of what? Exhaustion? Fear? I was not reading any of it very well.

I scooted as far as I could to my right and folded back the covers. She climbed in, rooted around to get comfortable, turned her back to me and started scooching my way. I had nowhere to go. I was hugging the edge of the bed as it were. I was surprised at myself. I'd fantasized about this, in great detail, every night for months and here I was, panicking. In my fantasy I was suave and self confident. Murmuring encouragement in a husky, sensuous tone of voice. Meanwhile back in reality I was on the verge of dropping my suave butt off the side of the bed. Go figure.

She finally scooched the width of the bed and nestled into me like a spoon. I was still being painfully uncooperative so she reached and pulled my left arm under her neck and my right arm over and around her waist.

I wasn't sure to what I owed the pleasure but I didn't want to do anything to cut it short. As a result, I was about as snuggly as a two by four.

As I calmed down and matched my breathing to hers I began to appreciate the position in which I found myself. I tightened my arms around her and pulled her against me and then struggled to keep my hands from roaming. As I laid my head back down against the pillow my lips came to rest against her neck and shoulders. I didn't know what her intentions were when she crawled into my bed but I assumed she had to know what she was doing to me. If she couldn't feel the rise and fall of my chest speeding up, she surely had to be able to hear me all but panting in her ear.

I breathed in her gentle fragrance and bit the inside of my cheek to make myself behave. But it was more than I could take. I gently kissed her behind the ear. When that got an 'mmmm' as a response I got bolder. I started to kiss slowly down her neck and across the back of her shoulder. She reached around and behind my neck with her right hand, wrapped her fingers in my hair and pulled me harder against her. Just to let her know I was paying attention, I bit down on the top of her shoulder. I was just about to roll her over and kiss her when I noticed she had gone from heavy breathing to soft crying.

What is it about me, I thought. Women always seem to cry in my arms. I was going to get a complex over it sooner or later.

"I'm sorry, Alex. I'm so sorry. I don't know what I was thinking. I don't know what I'm doing."

"I know what you were thinking and you were doing it quite well."

"I can't...I don't. I just wanted...I needed. Oh, God Alex. Just hold me."

So I did. I don't know how long we stayed like that but when things started heating back up for me I eased her away and turned her toward me.

"Talk to me. If nothing else is going to happen then we need to at least talk."

She took a deep breath and nodded her head. "My father had a stroke this morning. Yesterday morning. Whatever day it is. I've been at the hospital since seven. They got him stabilized late tonight and finally ran us all off, except Mama, around midnight. I don't know. I came home. I tried to sleep. I really did. But I just needed...I wanted...I...I had to be with you. I wasn't going to. But then I was in here. And I didn't mean for...but then I wanted it. And then I couldn't."

I watched the minutes click off the clock as we lay in silence.

"Marissa, I think you've probably picked up on it by now but in case you haven't I am one of the most patient and understanding people you will ever meet. But I've got to tell you something. You make me crazy."

"I know. And I'm sorry, I really am. I'm so confused. I don't know what I feel. Or what I want. I feel so comfortable with you. So comforted. Safe. Cared for. It's not fair to you. I know that. You give and ask for nothing. You don't push. I don't know what I'd do without you."

"Well, if it's up to me you won't have to find out. But Marissa, sooner or later you've got to decide where you stand on this. And then, well...stand there. I can't take much more back and forth stuff. I don't think it's any mystery how I feel. I can be friends if that's what you want. But I could also be so much more." I knew I shouldn't have but I gave it one more shot just in case. I reached around her, put my hand in the small of her back and started to pull us together. I felt her stiffen and start to fight it so I let her go.

I got her to hand me my shirt and shorts and we got up and made a pot of coffee. Not that I needed to be any more wound up than I already was. I felt like a piano wire. At the very least a high C. I'd had her in my bed. In my arms. I'd been kissing her and she'd responded. Forget the seeing things and hearing voices. This was what would eventually drive me mad. I couldn't come down from it. I knew if I closed my eyes I'd be able to relive every precious moment.

I stayed on the other side of the room while we talked. If she'd been within arms reach I couldn't have handled it. We'd crossed a boundary and I, for one, wasn't sure I could step back over it to where we had been before.

When morning rolled around she begged me to go to the hospital with her. I knew it was a mistake when I said yes, but there was no way I would have turned her down. I lectured myself the entire way there to keep my cool no matter what.

I don't do hospitals very well to begin with and as we pushed the door to the room open I could feel my chest tighten. Gathered around the bed were Mrs. Scafidi, Nick and Tony. They all looked up in unison. Mrs. Scafidi quickly dropped her eyes back to her husband.

"What the fuck!?"

"Don't start, Tony," Marissa snapped in a controlled whisper.

Nick moved to her side and said, "This is supposed to be family, 'Rissa." Marissa squared her shoulders. "Family is not always defined by blood, Nicky."

"Boys, why don't we go get something to eat and let Marissa have some time with Poppa." Mrs. Scafidi was doing her best to herd the two of them out of the room.

As Tony brushed past me he leaned over and said, "You're gonna regret this."

I couldn't let that slide. I briefly put a non-aggressive hand on his chest to stop him. In my most controlled tone I said, "This is neither the time nor the place. Your father…"

"*My father* would be saying the same fucking thing if he could talk without drooling all over himself. So don't tell me about *my* father."

"Alex."

"Tony."

The Scafidi women were trying to keep the peace. Marissa was tugging at me and her mother was tugging Tony in the opposite direction.

When we were alone I started to apologize but she beat me to it. "I'm sorry about Tony. He's a narrow-minded idiot. Just ignore him."

I didn't want to tell her that of all the idiots I'd ever encountered, the narrow minded ones were always the most dangerous. I stood off to the side while Marissa fussed over and talked to her father. It was hard to believe that the man in the bed was the same robust hulk of a man I'd seen in pictures of the family. He was in his early sixties, still worked a full day every day, drank, smoked, ate like a horse and could hold his own in a bar fight. He basically lived life with gusto according to Marissa. But then maybe that was what did it. There *is* something to be said for moderation.

She'd been talking nonstop for about thirty minutes when he suddenly tried to say something back to her. As she leaned closer to him she reached behind her back for me. I gave her my hand and she was pulling me towards her and the hospital bed when the door opened.

"Aw, Jesus Christ! I knew it! I just fuckin' knew it."

"Shut up, Tony. You don't know anything," Marissa turned on her brother and I dropped her hand and backed away.

About that time Nick, Mrs. Scafidi and the doctor came through the door. The focus mercifully switched to the doctor.

"Good news, good news. Our tests show that it's not as bad as we first thought. Mr. Scafidi has a long recovery period ahead of him but I see no reason, with rehabilitation of course, why he shouldn't regain all the functions of his left side. Walk, talk, eat…everything. Mind you, he won't be one hundred percent but he should get to the point where he can take complete care of himself."

Marissa had been holding her breath. She turned around towards Tony who was a few feet in front of me and to my left. She let out a huge sigh of relief and said, "Oh, thank God." She opened her arms and took a few steps forward. Tony opened his arms to hug her and she stepped past him and put her arms around my neck. I didn't respond immediately except to cut my eyes in Tony's direction. He was starting to turn red and a vein in his forehead was visibly throbbing. All I could think was, 'I'm dead. I'm dead. I'm dead.' Marissa squeezed tighter and more insistently so I hugged her back as Tony stormed out of the room.

The poor doctor looked totally confused. "Did I say something wrong?"

43

They took her father home a few days after that. It was a long and ardu-
ous process taking care of him, getting him to rehab and all but he was
a fighter and came along quicker than anyone, doctors included,
expected him to. Marissa spent a large majority of her time over there.
I understood but felt lonely and left out. We both decided it was better
that I stay out of it, though. My presence just seemed to upset everyone,
Tony in particular.

I also had my suspicions that Marissa was trying to put some distance between us. Unfortunately, I understood that, too. We had come
so close to making love. She had responded to me sexually. She had
come to my bed with that on her mind and it had almost happened. We
were still friendly. We were still close. But I had encouraged her to
decide where she stood and I was afraid she'd made her choice. It had
only been a few weeks, though, so I thought maybe I was jumping the
gun. In that day and age of sex at the drop of a hat, I didn't know if it
was refreshing or indicative of some deep underlying hang-up. I was
worried that almost a year's worth of foreplay, if it ever did happen,
would make it anti-climatic. No pun intended. I just tried to stay busy
and wait it out.

I've always liked to run in the wintertime. Well, actually, jog. Or
maybe an even more accurate description would be walk really fast
with a definite bounce in my step. Anyway, I'd started jogging daily at
the park, usually around dusk. I was working hard at filling my time

without Marissa. A few days before Thanksgiving I was finished with my run but still not ready to go back to an empty house. Even though it was fairly cold, there were a good many people out on the footpath so I veered off onto the less crowded bike path. I needed the solitude.

Most of my days lately had been filled with an internal argument. I was torn between sitting down with Marissa and getting it all out in the open or just trying to be patient and let things run their course. I'd never been very good at the 'whatever is meant to be, will be' philosophy. That was entirely too emotionally healthy for me. And it required a universal level of trust that I just couldn't seem to master. I'd done a lot of soul searching over the years and a great deal of reading. I knew the ins and outs of almost every religion known to man and had even ventured into the ancient mystery schools and esoteric writings. But as usual with me, my intellectual pursuits were lofty ideals and my life practices were, for the most part, the same as everyone else's. I could talk a good game and I could process events and ideas from a spiritual viewpoint but I got as mad and hurt, frustrated and discontent as the rest of the general population. Destiny, karma, 'whatever will be will be' were all very enticing concepts and probably quite true but I was as mistrustful of them as I was of the current societal norms.

I knew there had to be a happy medium. A balance of giving Marissa the space she needed but not pulling away or rejecting her for needing it. I wanted to remain emotionally consistent with her. If I shutdown because she shutdown then she might assume that she had nothing worth opening back up for. She'd seen me through a long month of hell and I needed to be as supportive as possible for her through this.

By the time I got to the end of the bike path and was turning around I had realized that my self concern and sense of loss had begun to interfere with my ability to support her and care for her while she went through this ordeal with her father. Everything did not have to revolve around me. I began to trot back to the Jeep with a renewed sense of hope and commitment.

I kept my head down, watching the path go by under my feet when I ran smack dab into someone's chest. I felt like a fool and began apologizing before I even regained my balance, until I heard them say, "Hello, Alex."

I looked up into Tony's face. It was not a welcome sight. "Not your usual path, but we managed to find you anyway." He glanced over my shoulder.

I whirled around and there was Nick walking up behind me. He didn't look as sure of himself or the situation as Tony did but he kept coming nonetheless. There was a moment where I could have run but it didn't register until it was gone.

I stood there trying desperately not to show the fear that was collecting at the base of my spine. It kills me to admit it but I'm talking about the burning stomach, acid in your veins, knee buckling kind of fear. I'd never even come close to experiencing that in the four years of gangs, drugs, guns and conscience-less killings of the neighborhood around the Center. I'd walked those streets many a night with not so much as a twinge.

Tony was advancing on me with his big meaty finger pointing in my face. I took a step backwards and felt myself press up against Nick. He didn't grab me or try to hold me and I had an idea he was not a particularly willing participant. Tony got close enough to start poking me hard on the chest. He leaned in further and I could see the individual splinters on the toothpick in his mouth.

"I'm only gonna tell you once. Stay the fuck away from my sister. I've been doing some talking with her and I don't like what I'm hearing. Or seeing. You're fillin' her head fulla shit she don't have no business thinking about. I'm taking care of her, though, don't you worry. Been going to Mass everyday. You got her so fucked up she's been scared to go to confession. Practically had to shove her in there the other day and she came out shakin' like a leaf. Bad enough you fucked with her head. But I *ever* find out you laid a hand on her, I'll kill you, you goddamned nigger lovin', atheist, commie pervert."

I could tell he was leaving one hell of a bruise on my chest and the pain from it was overriding the fear and beginning to piss me off. He seemed satisfied with his soliloquy and was probably about to turn and walk away. If I could have kept my mouth shut it would have all been over.

"Nigger lover, huh?" I could feel my blood boiling.

"Yeah."

"If you're talking about the kids I worked with, half of them were Hispanic, and I love them, too. If on the other hand, you're talking about my loving your sister, I wasn't aware she had any African American blood in her. But then, I don't pay any attention to those things." I had no idea until that moment that I harbored an unconscious death wish.

He backhanded me across the face so hard it spun me around to face Nick. Tony then reached under my arms and laced his fingers together behind my neck in a headlock.

"Go ahead Nicky, take a shot."

I took the opportunity offered by Nick's indecision to stomp on Tony's instep. I could only move my hands a few inches so I settled for raking the fingernails of both hands across his face as hard as I could. He screamed, grabbed my hand and bit it hard enough to draw blood and then threw me on the ground. I looked up expecting a foot to be coming my way, but saw Nick pointing down the bike path. The two of them took off running. I struggled to my feet about the time a couple rode up. They asked if I was OK and I told them yes, but to watch out for crazy people out there.

My face and hand throbbed but compared to being shot it amounted to the equivalent of a scratch. I walked back to the Jeep thinking that this had not been a good year for me.

When I took inventory in the rear view mirror I realized it was a little worse than I thought. My right eye was swelling shut and my cheek was already looking bruised. I was more concerned about my hand though. Human bites can be nasty things. I didn't want to think about what could have happened if that couple hadn't come along. Me and my big mouth. I stopped at a convenience store for some alcohol of the drinkable variety. The disinfectant could wait till I got home.

I could blow off most of the encounter as the false bravado of an ignorant coward. But the image of Marissa coming out of a confessional shaking like a leaf did not bode well for our budding relationship. A Billy Joel song flitted through my head and I rummaged in my tape case till I found the cassette with it on it. I popped it in and played it over and over on the way home.

Tony must have knocked me silly. Either that or my reduced drinking of late made those few beers go straight to my head. Instead of being angry or scared I found myself singing along. I was actually able to smile at the thought of Tony and his Catholic maneuverings. I was confident that I knew Marissa better than he did and while it might shake her up it wasn't going to work in the end. I decided I'd found my theme song. People looked at me like I was crazy. But I just threw my head back and sang. You know the one. It's got some great lines in it that seemed to fit.

I was putting Marissa's name in the song and singing, 'Come out Marissa don't make me wait...' That really made me smile.

It was so appropriate I can still recite it. I was singing when I pulled in the driveway. I hadn't counted on Marissa being home for a change. I tried to sneak into my side and get cleaned up but after making such a grand musical entrance I should have known better. She met me in the hall.

She had her hair up and was drying her hands on a red and white checked dishtowel. I realized how much her presence made that house feel like home. "I got home early and fixed dinner if you'd like to join me."

"Yeah. Sounds great. I've been running. Just let me get cleaned up." I was looking everywhere but at her. Not that there was anything I could do to hide it once we sat down to eat.

"Alex, what are you doing? Look at me." I turned to face her. "My God, what have you done now?"

I am so attuned to the subtleties in people. It might not have meant much to anyone else but I could tell by the changes in the way she phrased things that we were in trouble. A month before and it would have been 'Oh, my god, what happened? Are you okay? Let me help you.' Now it was 'what have you done now?' I was going to tell her the ugly truth of what happened but changed my mind at the last minute.

"A couple of guys jumped on me at the park. Looking for drug money I guess. I'm fine. No big deal."

"No big deal? Did you report it to the police?"

"No. By that time there was nothing anybody could have done. I didn't even get a good look at them."

She sighed heavily. "Honestly, Alex, you're just a magnet for this kind of thing. Well, come on, I'll help patch you up."

I was waiting for her to say 'again' but she didn't. There wasn't much to do for the shiner. There was no blood, no cuts, just one heck of a bruise. A little ice might take down some of the swelling but it was almost too late for that to be very effective. The bite on the hand didn't look as bad as I thought. There was broken skin in a couple of places but it could have been worse. While Marissa was boiling it out with peroxide she suddenly pulled my hand up close to her face.

"Oooo, gross. You didn't say you fought back."

I looked at her like I'd been caught in a lie. Imagine that. I shrugged and asked why.

"Because you've got half their skin under your fingernails. On both hands. No wonder they didn't stick around. They must have thought they'd jumped on a tiger." She laughed at that and I realized how little laughter I'd heard in the past few weeks. She wouldn't be laughing though if she knew whose skin it was.

We had a nice dinner. But it just wasn't the same as it used to be. I worked hard at telling funny stories and keeping the mood light but as soon as I would pause she'd sink back down. The little bit that she participated in the conversation seemed guarded and stiff. Occasionally she seemed to forget herself and enjoy the evening but then she'd reign herself back in. It was like she was putting forth a concerted effort to be a different person. I wondered if I was just being paranoid. Was she just tired and worried about her father, which she had every right to be? Or was there something else lurking beneath the surface. My gut usually wasn't wrong about those things.

She said she'd be going to her parents' for Thanksgiving lunch. I said that I'd cook during the day and we could have our Thanksgiving that night when she got home. She fiddled with the napkin in her lap and finally said she wouldn't be coming home. That she'd planned to stay over there through the weekend and go to work the next Monday from there. I suddenly had a very sick feeling about the dinner we were having that night. She was still staring at her lap and getting increasingly more nervous and fidgety. I'd been dumped before so I decided to save her the trouble of actually having to say it out loud. I couldn't sit there any longer. I apologized and excused myself before the meal was over. She jumped up, knocking her chair over in the process and chased me to the door.

I turned around with tears in my eyes and she reached down and held both my hands. The only thing that kept me going those next few months was that the look in her eyes said 'I love you' clear as day. When she spoke she said 'goodnight' but the agony in her eyes and the way she dropped her head clearly said the 'goodbye' that I was dreading.

I stepped into my side of the house. "If you want this door closed, you'll have to do it yourself. Oh, and Marissa, mizpah works both ways. When you're ready to come back I'll be here." I headed down the hall but then stopped and turned back to look at her. She had her hand on the doorknob and was slowly pulling it towards her. It was a cheap shot, but I added, "Until then, all I have to say is 'Baaaa.'" The stricken look on her face told me I'd hit home. I turned and walked the rest of the way down the hall and into my room, shutting the door behind me.

I wanted to believe she wasn't doing this of her own free will. Well, she was but she wasn't. She was folding under the pressure. If it had been what she really wanted then I wouldn't have had to suffer through listening to her sobs, and the occasional breaking of glass objects, into the wee hours of the morning. The next day when I got up I found the connecting door a little more than halfway closed.

44

"God, Alex, I've got to stop. Hand me those Kleenex."

"Aw come on, Sharon, I would have thought you'd heard and seen it all by now."

"Maybe it's because I know you so well or maybe it's the way you tell it, but it's playing out in front of my eyes like a movie. For crying out loud, you've taken me from almost blowing some kid's head off, through crippling depression, to a budding relationship, a beating and a breakup in a few hours. I can't take anymore tonight."

"But it gets better. I promise."

"It'll have to get better tomorrow, then. I can't take another install-ment tonight. Maybe I should rethink making you talk about the hard stuff."

Marissa

Part Two

45

Wednesday June 9, 1999 10:00AM

"Marissa, when are you due? I feel like I should be boiling water before our sessions just in case."

"Oh no, don't worry about that. I've got another month to go. I just *look* like I'm about to explode. How's Alex?"

"Alex is fine. Exhausting, but fine."

"I know all about that. Talk about longwinded."

"Yes, most assuredly. Normally I'd be getting frustrated with a client that took this long to fill me in. But I have to admit I'm hooked and not being very objective. The two of you should write a book. If I didn't already know that it ends with the two of you committed to working it out, *I'd* be going crazy right about now. What a story."

"Yes it is, isn't it? That's why we've got to fix it before the baby gets here."

"Well then let's get started. My notes say we left off with Carlos' murder. Alex brought me up to Thanksgiving of that year. Start wherever you like but I'm particularly interested in your reaction to Alex's birthday revelation."

46

You know the line at the beginning of Tale of Two Cities? 'They were the best of times. They were the worst of times'? That period from the shooting at City Hall all the way through that winter was like that for us. If we could have just shut out the rest of the world. But it kept creeping back in. I know what they mean by a fighter being punch drunk now. Every time we'd recover from one blow and have a period of peace and happiness, something else would happen that rocked our world.

We've been through so much. You don't even know the half of it. When Alex used to talk about our being soul mates, I thought it was nonsense. But I believe it now. I can't *not* be with Alex. Every part of my being cries out for it. I'd be dead inside if we weren't together. I don't know why I ever thought differently. But I did. And I've done some stupid things as a result.

When Alex finally pulled out of the depression over Carlos, I felt like I'd been given a reprieve from a death sentence. We had a wonderful summer after that. It was as if we were making up for lost time. I suddenly had a new awareness of how precious it all was. I felt like a butterfly finally released from the confines of my cocoon. Literally alive for the first time. I wanted to see it all, feel it all. Taste it, hear it, sense it. And Alex. God, Alex was like a magnifying glass, an amplifier.

Everything was brighter, darker, hotter, colder, louder, softer. It was like a whole world existed that I'd never been part of. I had feelings I'd only read about or seen in movies. It sounds crazy but it's true.

The only thing that would stop me in my tracks is when I would think; 'this is what it's like to be in love'. It would hit me at the oddest times and I'd look at Alex and wonder, 'is that what this is'? I would lay in bed at night staring at these glow in the dark stars over my bed and wonder what it would be like to be lying in the next room looking at the one's over Alex's bed.

Although Alex would be the first to tell you that I have quite successfully worked through it, at the time there was no other word to describe me sexually but repressed. Half the time just the thought of lying next to Alex would panic me and I'd be physically withdrawn for days afterward. But then some nights, lubricated so to speak with a little wine, I could imagine sneaking next door and waking Alex up with unexpected kisses. My fantasies never could make it past the kissing stage but even that could make me feel jelly-kneed. Successful fantasy nights would make me a little bolder the next day. I'd be more physically attentive but when I'd get a response, and I always got a response, I'd freeze up.

Then I'd start questioning everything. What was I doing attracted to someone like Alex? Believe me, none of it fit my preconceived notions of romance, love or relationships. There was too much equality. I had a voice, a say in things. I was not only allowed but even encouraged to go and do and be. In my book that's friendship, not love. I knew Alex cared deeply about me but in love with me? Not hardly. I was fooling myself on that one. When someone's in love with you they want to know where you go, what you do, who you talk to. Don't scowl at me. That's all I'd ever seen growing up. It's all I knew.

I'd be on the verge of giving myself over to it in spite of my reservations. To hell with family and friends, who were they to tell me what was right for me? But then I'd talk myself out of it telling myself there was no future for us so why would I give the most precious part of me away?

And yet I couldn't completely dismiss it. Every time I got near Alex, every time we touched it was like an electrical current went through me. There was a familiarity there that didn't make any sense. Sometimes I would forget that we hadn't ever made love. On one hand I knew exactly what it would be like and on the other hand I hadn't a clue. It was the most confusing time of my life. I can't tell you how many times I stood in the doorway to that room watching Alex sleep, unable to take another step forward but not able to turn around and leave either.

If there was an awareness on Alex's part of what I was going through it was never mentioned. I got the message loud and clear that nothing was going to happen unless *I* made it happen.

Other than the constant late night torture of my indecision, life was grand. We spent every waking, non-working moment together that we could. I can look back at it now and realize that we were doing the get-to-know-you dance that's usually done in the serious monogamous dating stage of a relationship. But since I still wasn't willing to call it a relationship at the time, I just thought of it as being extremely and conveniently compatible.

Which is another reason why it came as such a surprise to discover a huge piece of Alex that I knew nothing about.

47

I knew Alex had an aversion to birthdays for some reason. I had to do the 'dig in the billfold and sneak a peek at the driver's license' routine just to find out the date. I wanted it to be a surprise but not over-whelming. I had no idea about the family situation but knew they were all here in Mississippi. So that was out of the question even if I'd felt like it would have been well received. Then I thought of the kids at the Center. Alex hadn't been able to spend much quality time with them all summer but hadn't avoided them either. I knew they were missed, so that idea felt safe. Just a few of the favorites and a quiet evening of pizza, cake and ice cream.

It was comical at first but got tedious the longer we waited. Alex was hours late getting home. The pizza was gone in ten minutes. The chitchat was exhausted in thirty. I hardly knew these kids and they didn't want to spend their evening with some uptight attorney. They wanted to see Alex. They turned on a ballgame and got in a heated argument. They made themselves more at home than I was comfortable with and cranked up my stereo and practically cleaned out my refrigerator. That was about the time they discovered my wine rack and the beer in the back of the fridge. I told them no, they were under age and they looked at me like I was from another planet. I figured what the heck, it could either settle them down or make me where I, at least, didn't care.

About an hour after that Alex got home and we had a nice little sur-prise party and played cards and talked for hours. I was much more accepted in Alex's presence than I was by myself. The conversation turned to birthdays in general. Where everybody was born, what hospital, how much they weighed, who they looked like. I noticed Alex not only not participating but also starting to toss the beers back one after another. When I realized things were beginning to go downhill I got up and started cleaning as a signal the party was over. The kids picked up on it immediately and left. We cleaned up and Alex opened my present.

Over the summer we'd gotten so close and open with each other that nothing was off limits discussion wise so I just waded right in.

"Alex, what's wrong?"

"Nothing."

"Yes there is."

"No there's not."

"Why are you acting this way?"

"I'm tired."

"Maybe so, but it doesn't explain your mood."

"Yes it does."

"No it doesn't."

"Leave me alone. I'm going to bed."

"Oh no you're not. I have learned from the master of personal inquisition. So sit down, 'master', and start talking."

"Marissa. Go fish."

"Go fish yourself." Which, thank god always made us laugh. It only got a smile this time so I knew it was serious but Alex did sit down and looked resigned to the inevitable.

"So what's with the birthday aversion?" I asked. I didn't expect the hostile, sarcastic tone of voice I got in return.

"Well, let's see. Birthday celebrations ultimately are designed to celebrate the original event. Right? It's not so much that you survived another year. Which in my case would be cause to celebrate given what all has happened. But the conversation, just like tonight, always seems to end up on the original one. And childhood. You get to play the what did you look like, who'd you take after game.

Well, you know what? I don't know. I don't know where I was born, other than Louisiana. I don't know what parish, what town, what hospital. If I was even born in a hospital at all. Could have been a house, could have been the backseat of a '57 Chevy for all I know. Which is probably where I was conceived so that would be appropriate, don't you think? I don't know who to. Okay!? Don't know exactly what I looked like. Certainly don't know *who* I looked like. Where'd I get my size, shape, hair, eyes, nose? *I don't know*!

There's no one in my family whose face I can look at and say, 'hey, there's me'. I don't fit, Marissa. I don't fit anywhere. Well that's not true. I must fit somewhere. I just don't know where the hell that is. Well, no, now that I think about it I was right the first time. I don't fit anywhere because they obviously didn't want me. So I don't know."

Alex had popped off the couch at the first 'I don't know' and had been pacing ever since. I'd seen the soapbox persona many times when discussing politics or injustice in general. But this was hurt, angry, vehement, resentful. I was sitting in the big stuffed chair and Alex walked over, grabbed each arm of the chair and leaned down in my face. I never admitted that I was scared but I was.

"Do you understand what I'm saying? *I DON'T KNOW!*"

I was leaning as far back as I could and said in as neutral a tone as I could muster, "Alex, back up, please." There was an expression of realization and I was able to sit up straight again. Then the pacing started all over. "And no, I'm not exactly sure *what* you're trying to tell me."

"I was given up, as they call it. Not wanted, I call it. Don't have a clue who my biological parents were. I guess I was a mistake, or not the right model, or was going to be too much trouble. There aren't even any pictures of me until I was over a year old. Cause, you see, I wasn't even adopted right away. I got to hang around in an orphanage for a year. Sickly baby. No one wants the burden of adopting a baby with health problems. Not when there are so many of us and they can have the pick of the litter."

"Oh, Alex…"

"Well sure. My Mom and Dad used to tell me, 'I wasn't expected, I was selected'. But over the course of a year, how many families *didn't* select me? Huh? Think about *that*."

I decided this was no time to try and sound reasonable or soothing. I just let it play itself out.

"Don't give me that tsk, tsk look. I know how it sounds. You're getting the worst of it. But then you asked for it don't forget. I was in therapy for it the whole time I was in grad school. Didn't go in for that but it seemed that's what all my problems boiled down to. Sharon, my therapist, calls it abandonment issues. Three hundred sixty four days a year I either don't think about it at all or handle it pretty well, depending on whether or not those rejection buttons get pushed. But birthdays…"

"Alex, I'm sorry. I didn't know I was bringing all this up for you. I had no idea."

"You didn't bring it up. It was already there. You just brought it out. I know you had no idea and I feel bad about that. It's just not something I talk about."

"There's more isn't there?"

"Well yeah, but it's just about being maladjusted, paranoid and perfectionistic. Nothing important."

That comment was followed by a sarcastic chuckle and Alex came and sat on the floor in front of me, leaned back against my legs and started talking. Less agitated and more of a painful, matter of fact monotone, but I got a good bit more of the story.

"I stayed in the orphanage for a year. Very sick. Probably a low birth weight baby of a teenaged mother. But who knows? You know, when you're not snatched up immediately by a new family and it looks like you're going to be around for awhile they have to give you a name. They can't just call you Baby 487-255 forever. Infants and toddlers don't respond very well to that.

Do you know why babies these days are immediately put on the mother's stomach as soon as they're born? It's called the mother bond. That baby in the uterus for nine months has come to know everything there is to know about that mother. Heartbeat, warmth, stomach sounds, breath sounds, emotions, electrostatic charges, voice, everything. They put that baby on the mother's stomach so that it immediately know it's all right, it's still safe, it's still with Mom. The baby is okay being in a wildly different environment because, hey, Mom's still here.

Think what it must be like to be suddenly ripped from the cozy, sloshy place you've called home for nine months, squeezed through this relatively small canal out into the bright, noisy, cold world; get smacked on the butt and then...no Mom. Nothing familiar. Newborns can't talk but just think what they must be feeling.

Then you hang out in the hospital a couple of days. Nurses check on you. You get fed and changed. But nobody holds and cuddles and snuggles you. Not like a Mom would. There is no crowd of people peeking at you and waggling their fingers at you through the viewing window. There is no one.

Then if you don't already have a family waiting for you, you go to the orphanage or maybe foster care. Where I was headed with this earlier before I got sidetracked was that if you're at the orphanage long enough, they give you a name. And like all babies, you begin to connect that word with all the times that someone is paying attention to you, so you begin to like that word, that name. Eventually you realize that that word *is* you. Even at that age, your identity is forming. Then sooner or later, for me it was later, some family adopts you. But they don't like that name, aka they don't like you, so they change it. So you're suddenly not you anymore. Presto, chango, you are now the you that *they* want you to be. Not the you that you were.

And somehow you get it in your little bitty head that in order to be sure that these people don't also give you up or trade you in, you better learn to always be exactly what they want you to be. Not who you really are. Because you've already learned that being who you really are obviously doesn't work. I mean, think about it. You've bonded with the person that gave you life and carried you around for nine months, but they got rid of you. Then you bond with and depend on the people in the hospital but for some reason they get rid of you. Then you cling to and bond with the people in the orphanage that take care of you but in the end they get rid of you, too. So by that time you figure you better do whatever it takes to not be gotten rid of anymore.

So you learn to be perfect. Not just perfect, but the perfect chameleon. The pressure to be exactly what everyone wants you to be is enormous, especially for a child. I had ulcers by the time I was eight. I had panic attacks if I didn't make straight A's. I practiced every sport imaginable until I would almost drop dead so that I would be the best player on the best team. And not only be a member of every club and honor society but an officer, preferably the president.

And it worked! Everybody thought I was the best at everything. They thought I had it all. I was worth keeping. I was the only one who knew the truth. I was the only one who knew that the real me was just worthless. Nothing. The only skill I really had was like the Chinese troupe at the circus who could keep all those plates spinning at the same time."

We sat there awhile. My head was pounding. What can you say to that? So I simply asked, "What about your adoptive parents?"

"The McKinley's? Wonderful people. I was so damn lucky. Loving. Caring. Pure hearts of gold. Shirt off their backs kind of folks. Well respected. God fearing. Don't smoke, don't drink, don't curse. Hard working. Protective. Strict. There were a few nuts on the branches of the family tree but Mom and Dad are solid.

I love my parents more than I can say. More than they'll ever know. I really sold them short during my teenaged years when I started thinking and feeling all this consciously. I blamed them for my fears, paranoia and rejection issues. Because they *did* have incredibly high, almost unachievable, expectations of me. I didn't realize until therapy that I had set them up to have those expectations because I came out of the starting block acting like the perfect overachieving child. The motivation for my perfectionism, the fear of being given up, was so unconscious, so deeply buried in my psyche, that all I knew as a child was that they sure seemed to expect me to be perfect. And during those awful, angst filled teenaged years I not only blamed them for it, I started rebelling. A little in high school. A whole lot in college.

We're still estranged because of it all. I brought shame on the family in more ways than you could keep track of. Of course there were some family members who would whisper behind their hands that it was no surprise, really, because everybody knows Alex doesn't actually have any McKinley blood in the veins. Let me tell you, that hurt.

What I was really doing was trying on most every behavior, thought and feeling I could in order to find the ones that fit the real me. I'd reached a point where I wanted to know who I was. I did it in an angry and unhealthy way but I was still young and stupid in the way that twenty-year-olds just naturally are.

I smoked, I drank, I cursed, I tried drugs. I changed my major from a respectable pre-med biochemistry to psychology. According to my Dad, aspiring to be nothing more than someone who messes with other people's heads. I skipped classes. I flunked classes. I lost my scholarships. I dropped out of college my junior year. When none of that felt like me I began exploring new ways of thinking and believing spiritually. I quit going to church and that almost killed them, staunch Southern Baptists that they are. And don't even mention the type of girlfriends I had. I wasn't allowed to bring anybody within a fifty-mile radius of Tupelo.

Things did improve for awhile. I finally realized that for the most part I *was* the person I'd always been. I was smart, a good student, a good athlete, popular. I just needed to be myself without worrying whether or not anyone else liked it. So I got my act together. I quit smoking, cigarettes *and* pot. Went back to school and finished my degree with straight A's my senior year. Went on to grad school and got my Masters in Social Work. Straight A's again. The less I felt like I *had* to do well the easier it was.

That seemed to impress my Mom and Dad so they didn't mind when I moved back to Tupelo and took the job as director of the General Crisis Center. They were actually proud. Until that ended in the biggest scandal Tupelo had seen in a long time. Remember Jessie? Which is what brought me here. They practically disowned me for that one. I see them at Christmas and talk to them occasionally.

So, all that should now explain why I am the perfectionistic, anal retentive, paranoid, relationship ruining, take everything personally, people pleasing person that I am. *Now* can I go to bed?"

Alex was still leaning against my knees. I tapped that cute, cowlicked head and when it tipped backwards I bent and kissed it. On the forehead, not the lips, although I wanted to. Actually, what I saw and felt was a little child that needed to be scooped up and held and rocked until the boo boo inside healed. I had cried silent crocodile tears off and on through the whole story. What I wanted to say more than anything was, 'I love you. *I* do. Nobody else matters anymore, because I love you and always will'.

But I knew even though I meant it from the deepest part of my soul, Alex would view it at that precise moment as a profession of love born of pity. So I kept my mouth shut. Problem is, I continued to feel it but never managed to say it after that.

We just sat there until the sun came up which wasn't that much longer. When we finally said goodnight, or goodmorning rather, I spent several hours lying in my bed wanting to go join Alex just to cuddle, to soothe, and wondering if I should. Or if I'd even be welcome after opening up that emotional wound.

48

We danced around each other for a few days afterward but things went back to normal soon enough. Actually they were better than they were before. I felt like another layer of that onion had been peeled away and we were even closer. We spent the next few months traveling all over the countryside on the weekends going to fairs and festivals and antique shows.

I wasn't able to embrace it for what it was, an intense intimate love relationship that simply had yet to be consummated physically. And because of that I really missed out in a lot of ways. I remember every detail of everything we did together but it got labeled in my brain as 'all the fun things I did with my good buddy Alex'. I can go back in my mind now and relive it knowing what came later but the experiences themselves would have been so much more meaningful if I could have allowed myself take it to that next level. We could have held hands and fed each other cotton candy and licked each other's fingers clean. We could have bought antiques for *us* instead of for ourselves. We could have made love in front of the fireplaces in the rooms at the inns we stayed in. It was wonderful but it could have been so much more. I still feel guilty for holding us back. But everything supposedly happens for a reason, don't you think? I'm not sure what that reason was but I keep telling myself it was meant to happen exactly the way it did. Although there were parts I would have gladly skipped.

For example, like I said earlier, after some peace and happiness something else always seemed to come along and knock us down. This next one actually knocked us out. It was sometime in November and I was moping around the house early one morning. I never slept very well in the house by myself and Alex was out of town on business. I grabbed the phone on the first ring hoping to hear that my wayward housemate was coming home early. Hearing Nick's voice before six o'clock in the morning made my heart stop. As if on cue he told me Pop had been rushed to the hospital after Mama found him lying on the bathroom floor.

I didn't wait to hear anymore. I hung up the phone while he was still talking and ran down the hall. I threw on some clothes and flew to the hospital. Not that there was anything I could do when I got there. We all sat and paced, paced and sat for the majority of the day. Every time the doors would swing open we'd all leap up only to find that it wasn't his doctor. They let Mama go back and see him in between tests but the rest of us had to wait it out. It was late that afternoon before we were told that he'd had a stroke and possibly a heart attack and it was several more hours before they got him into a Cardiac Care room. Tony was huffing and puffing and threatening to blow the hospital down but they'd heard it all before and just ignored him. When he found he couldn't bully the hospital staff he took it out on Nick and I.

So all in all it could not have been a more miserable day. All I wanted was to see my father and to have Alex there to lean on and to tell me everything would be all right. They started allowing us to see him one at a time for ten minutes every hour. Mama went first, then me; Tony then Nick. I got to see him a second time around eleven o'clock. He was asleep both times I went in which was probably good. Tony said Pop had tried to talk to him but couldn't get his mouth to work right and got very upset. By midnight the doctor felt he was stable enough to move him to a private room which would allow Mama to spend the night. We had the choice of sleeping in the waiting room or going home. Tony, being the oldest male child, decided he would be the one to stay and that since Nick and I both lived close we'd go home. I wasn't about to say so out loud but it suited me fine because all I wanted was Alex. Things had been so crazy I hadn't even called.

When I got home and all the lights were off, I told myself it could wait until morning. I took a shower and tried to sleep. I tossed and turned, this way and that. I cried and I squirmed. I felt guilty because thoughts of Pop were not what was on my mind. I decided, regardless of the time, I had to talk to Alex. But I still hesitated. It didn't feel quite right for some reason. I forced myself to lie still and just feel. That's when I realized I didn't need to talk to Alex. I needed to *feel* Alex. The strength, the safety, the protectiveness, the love that I knew was there. I needed to be held. I needed those arms around me. I needed…I wasn't sure what else I needed. But I knew where I could find it.

I got up and tip toed to Alex's doorway. There was enough light coming through the blinds to see tousled hair and bare shoulders. I'd been at that threshold so many times before. But this time I stepped through the door and up to the bed. I could feel myself start breathing harder. Nervousness or desire? Hard to tell. Alex woke up and since there was no where to hide I stammered that I wanted to sleep in there.

Can you imagine? The gallant idiot starts talking about getting up and sleeping on the couch. Sharon, I had to spell it out. And I don't know what I expected when I got under the covers but it definitely was not to be surrounded by nothing but cold air.

Poor Alex was doing everything possible to *not* touch me. But then I wasn't completely committed to it in my own head so I suppose I was guilty of giving off mixed signals. I slid all the way to the other side of the bed before I felt skin. There was that mysterious electric current and familiarity again. But no real response from Alex. My initial thought before I went in there was that it would take some effort on my part to keep things just cuddly if that really was all I wanted, but I was beginning to wonder if I was the only repressed one here. I had to pull one arm and then the other around me. We lay there a moment and it soon got difficult to tell which one of us was breathing harder. I was confused, though, because Alex was still holding back. I started having second thoughts until I felt my body start to take over. I thought, 'Oh god what am I doing? What ever possessed me to think that all I wanted was just closeness and comfort?'

I couldn't keep myself still. My body wanted Alex to know what it wanted. Then I felt hot rapid breathing on the back of my neck and the most tender, sensual, slow kiss. I tried not to react but it was impossible. I clamped my teeth together but moaned in spite of myself.

That tiny affirmation was all it took. I was suddenly in the arms of a different person. This person knew exactly what they wanted and what they were doing. The timidity and lack of confidence was gone. Something about that single kiss dissolved all the boundaries I'd worked so hard to maintain. There was no doubt in my mind I was with a lover that knew all the secrets and would take plenty of time sharing them. And it scared me to death.

That feeling of fear tapped into the fear I'd been experiencing all day at the hospital and then, of all things, an image of my father popped into my head. I started to cry.

I have never been so embarrassed in my life. True to form, Alex didn't get angry or try to push it. We just lay there holding each other. I do remember being gently told that sooner or later I was going to have to decide what I wanted. And I got the first spoken confirmation that Alex wanted more than friendship.

Neither one of us could lie there in that bed any longer. Fear or no fear, the desire was there. It would have started again and even though my body was saying yes, some part of me was obviously not ready. So we got up and talked the rest of the night.

49

Everything went to hell after that. Or maybe I should say I got convinced that was where I would be going. It all spun out of control so quickly I didn't have time to think. I just reacted. Or maybe I thought too much. If I'd been seeing you then you probably would have had me committed I was acting so crazy.

When we went to the hospital the next day Alex and Tony had words with each other and Tony stormed out of the room. I also began freaking out over being so forward as to crawl in bed with Alex the night before. I just knew it was written all over my face. Good girls don't do that, you know. So I was ripe for all the crap that my brother started feeding me.

I was going to my parents' house every day after work to help with Pop. Taking care of him was a twenty-four hour a day job at first. The boys would sit with him, talk to him and help bathe him but that was about it. I helped Mama with the cooking, cleaning, laundry, and grocery shopping. Just generally giving her a break so she could get some sleep. In all fairness to Tony and Nick, they *were* working overtime to keep the family plumbing business together in Pop's absence, but I resented the obvious delineation between what was men's work and what was women's work. To Tony that was a sign that I'd been around 'Alex the liberal' too long.

It soon became painfully obvious that Tony thought any time with Alex was too much time. He started in on me the first night I was there and never let up. Told me he was speaking for the whole family, which I found out much later wasn't true.

I didn't think Tony was bright enough to be that manipulative. When I look back with a clear head I can see how well planned and thought out it was. If he had simply said terrible things and insisted I stay away from Alex, it would have only served to solidify our relationship. But instead, he slowly chipped away at me, pushing every button I had. Pulling on every Catholic and family guilt-laden string.

I didn't realize how much ammunition I'd given him. I thought I had been fairly tight lipped about our friendship but I must have talked about us a lot more than I remembered.

Tony told me that he thought Alex had been stalking me after we were trapped together in the elevator. He wanted to know what I thought the chances were of our ending up in the same house out of all the possible houses in the entire city. He believed Alex had followed me and rented the other side as soon as I rented mine. I told him that was ridiculous. The landlord had told me that the other side had been rented out the week before. Tony said maybe that wasn't Alex. Maybe Alex paid off the landlord to turn the original renter down.

Night after night it was something new. How our picture in the paper after the shooting had embarrassed the family, being such an inappropriate public display. And then to turn around and be caught on TV, the only two white people at a black gang banger's funeral. Holding hands no less. He said they'd had to fend off questions from the priest on down when they went to Mass. According to him I had brought shame on the family.

I was already so shaken up by the combination of Pop's illness and my brief but intense sexual reaction to Alex that I couldn't think straight. It didn't dawn on me as this continued that Tony knew way more than he should have.

He knew about our using both sides of the house and how we were always together everywhere. Of course he didn't say he knew. He phrased it as questions, implying that he could guess how things had progressed. He said he bet Alex had a hard time at first getting me to be friends. And then it slowly built from there, more and more time together, more and more things in common. My overall confusion and vulnerability made me fertile ground for seeds of doubt.

I can't tell you how my head was reeling from all of this. He fed it to me a little at a time and then left me to think about it. Was it true? Was he right? It all fit. He said that out of concern for me he'd talked to our priest. He wanted me to start going to Mass with him every day and to talk to Father Matthew. He harped a lot on Alex not only not being Catholic but not being religious at all.

Tony was obsessed with getting me away from Alex. He punctuated every nightly lecture with the same thing, 'Marissa, you've got to think of your family. Alex just isn't our kind of people'.

I fell right into it. I did start going to Mass. Every day. I'd always found answers at church before. And it felt comfortable to turn there again. I hadn't been to confession in a long time and didn't want to face that part of it. Tony practically shoved me in the confessional one evening. Father Matthew was patient and understanding at first in order to get me talking. I could tell, though, that he'd heard and believed Tony's version already. That old confession behavior kicked in and I let it all pour out. Lust and love and desire and confusion. I was emotionally exhausted when I stepped out. I'd gotten my answer. It wasn't the one I wanted.

I skipped going to my parents' the next night and went home. It was almost Thanksgiving and Alex and I had made plans for the long weekend. I wanted to be fair and not drag it out any longer. It just wasn't going to work and we needed to break it off before anything else happened. Maybe in time we could go back to just being friends.

There was no easy way to do it. Particularly since I didn't want to. My heart was broken into so many pieces it felt like I had crushed glass in my chest. You said you'd gotten to Thanksgiving with Alex so I'm sure

you know the details. I have never, ever hurt like that and it was com-
pounded at the end by being bleated at like a sheep. I would have preferred for Alex to walk up and slap me across the face. After all, I felt I
deserved it. But the 'Baaa'? That was like a knife through my heart.
Because I knew deep down, it was true.

I was suddenly experiencing firsthand, the kind of grief Alex must
have felt for Carlos. Everything in my life went back to being dull and
meaningless. Nothing was alive anymore. Everything was dead.
Through it all I managed, somehow, to convince myself I'd done the
right thing. For both of us. For everyone concerned.

I suppose if you know all that, then you know who jumped on Alex
at the park. There aren't any words for the horror I felt over that. And
to find that Alex had protected them, knowing full well that Tony was
committed to driving us apart. The love I had forced myself to lock
away came flooding back in a torrent.

Tony must have assumed that Alex had spilled the beans the day it
happened, because he didn't try to hide it. As a matter of fact he was so
proud of it that he answered the door when I arrived for Thanksgiving
dinner. He and I both bent over at the same time to pick up my bags,
since I was staying through the weekend. When we almost bumped
heads, we stopped to look at each other, our faces only inches apart. He
was grinning from ear to ear, and down both sides of his face were
scabbed over claw marks. I blinked and looked again. The realization
slowly crawled through me like ice water.

"You son of a bitch!" I slapped him across the face as hard as I could.

He laughed. "You shouldn't call Mama names now, sis."

"You son of a bitch!" I said again and took another swing at him but
he grabbed my wrist and bent it backwards.

"I just wanted to make our position very clear in case you chick-
ened out."

"Well I didn't. But I'm going to correct that mistake right now." I
turned to leave and he jerked me back.

"Where do you think you're going?"

"Home. To Alex. Where I belong."

"You do and there won't be anything left to patch up next time. So get your butt in here and give thanks for having a family that looks after you and protects you from yourself."

He pulled me inside the house, threw my bags in behind me and slammed the door.

I suffered through dinner picking at my food. When it was over I excused myself immediately, saying I felt sick, not even helping with the dishes. I stayed locked in my room the entire weekend only coming out to help Mama when I was sure Tony wasn't there. I didn't know what I should do. I felt like I'd been sentenced to solitary confinement. And now I had the added incentive of Tony's threat to consider.

I was curled up in a ball on the bed on Saturday evening when there was a very light tapping on my door. Mama always gave a hearty yell from whatever room she was in and Tony tended to beat on doors so I knew it must be Nicky.

I let him in, lay down again and curled back up. He sat on the edge of the bed and rubbed my back.

"Are you mad at me?"

"Yes, Nicky, I'm mad at you. Did you think I wouldn't be?"

"I wasn't sure. I thought maybe you knew I didn't feel the same way as Tony."

"And how was I supposed to know that, Nick? Alex said there were two guys. You went with him to the park, didn't you?"

"Yeah but I didn't do anything. He made me go. You know how he gets."

"Oh, so he dragged you there kicking and screaming against your will and forced you to participate?"

"Well, no. It was more like how he got you to change your mind about Alex when you didn't want to."

He hung his head in embarrassment. I knew the feeling all too well. His words were so true they stung. We were both allowing a big bully to jerk us around like rag dolls.

"So what are we going to do about it?"

"I don't know, 'Rissa. To be honest, I'm afraid of him."

I felt sorry for Nicky. Here was this sweet, loving, gentle soul wrapped up in this big, strapping body, stuck in a family that expected their men to be brutish. He'd learned not to let his soft side show, but I knew it was in there. I reached up and patted his cheek.

"You know, 'Rissa, I don't know much of anything about Alex. But I do know you've been really happy for the first time in as long as I can remember since you guys started hanging out together."

"Thank you. At least somebody sees that. I know it's probably hard for you to understand." I sighed and sat up. "Yes, Alex has dramatically changed my life. But Nick, it *needed* changing, if that makes any sense."

"I understand that better than you think," he said. He patted my arm, got up and left.

While I wasn't entirely sure I had a staunch ally, it was nice to know my entire family was not my enemy. Not that it mattered that much. I hated Tony's tactics but at the time I believed he was right in one respect. There would never be a happily ever after for Alex and I. In the end we were entirely too different. So what was the point in trying, only to be disappointed and hurt? On the other hand, how do you know for sure if you don't get the opportunity to give your all? I went in circles like that to a greater or lesser degree all the way to March.

50

"Does this mean we're about to make it to 1997 in less than two total hours?"

"No wonder Alex likes you. You're very sarcastic, Sharon."

"It's just that in my best estimate Alex is averaging about a month an hour."

"I think you should count yourself lucky that it's going that quickly."

"Isn't that the truth? Before we wrap up today, tell me about the time while you and Alex were, for the lack of a better word, separated."

"It was horrible. I don't know how else to describe it. I've never felt so alone, so isolated in my life."

"Describe it for me."

51

Well, I knew I had to go home sooner or later and learn to be near Alex, but not close to Alex. It was miserable. When you're dating someone and break it off, the grief period is usually time limited and then you go on with your life. But that's because you don't see that person anymore. At least not on a daily basis. And not in the same environment in which your relationship developed.

I can't explain how it felt to have the person that I had become accustomed to eating, talking, laughing, crying, arguing, traveling, shopping, working, and living with; to have that person on the other side of a half open door, day in and day out. To know that all I had to do at any moment was step through that door and give myself to Alex completely and my pain would disappear.

But that was the catch. 'Give myself completely'. I suddenly realized that all of this was *not* about Tony, or threats, or family, or religion, or coming from different worlds. It was about my inability to love and be loved. It had nothing to do with sex, either. This went much, much deeper. Making love was merely symbolic of being able to lower my defenses and welcome Alex inside my heart, mind, soul and body. Until I could give all four of those freely and completely I owed it to Alex to stay away. I knew it had to be all or nothing and since my ability to give it all had been taken from me years before, I resigned myself to nothing.

At first we avoided each other like the plague. Then it got to where we could speak when we saw each other. We plateaued there for almost a month. I say we. It was more along the lines of I established the boundary and Alex quietly honored it.

The only time it was crossed was at Christmas. God, Sharon, that house was so sad. It was the only one in the neighborhood that had no decorations whatsoever. If anything, it looked like a house of mourning, which I suppose it was.

I got up early Christmas day to get ready to go suffer through the 'family thing'. As I was leaving I found a small gift box set just inside that damned half open door. I picked it up and debated what I should do, what the right thing to do was. I decided to hell with that, this might be the last gift I ever get from Alex. I took it back to my room and nervously opened it.

Lying on a piece of velvet was a beautiful gold necklace with a pendant. When I looked closer, I saw that the pendant was actually one half of a broken heart. When I looked closer yet, I saw an indentation on the velvet where a larger chain with the other half of the heart had been.

I took it out, closed the box and clasped it to my chest. I slowly slid off the bed and onto the floor. Dissolving into tears, I rocked back and forth like an autistic child murmuring 'Alex, Alex, Alex'…over and over. When I was finally able to stand up, I put the necklace on and left it on the outside of my blouse. I wore it like that to my parents' house and when Tony saw it I know the look in my eyes dared him to say something.

He'd invited one of his buddies from the neighborhood to join us. He'd been doing an awful lot of that lately. Every time he knew I was going to be there as a matter of fact. The scenarios had gotten so predictable that it would have been humorous if it didn't make me sick. These boys, I wouldn't even call them men, were always self absorbed, arrogant idiots who followed me around the house like puppies trying to get my attention. When that didn't work they'd go back to drinking with the guys in the living room until they got drunk enough and bold enough to search me out and try to corner me in some secluded room in the house. Half the time I couldn't tell if they were trying to grope me or just hold their drunken selves up. Either way it was disgusting.

Christmas day was no different except I got up the nerve to excuse myself very early and go home. When I got home the Jeep was gone. I came in and sat at the kitchen table with my head in my hands. It was impossible not to compare all those guys to Alex. I mulled the latest one over, and while he was cute enough and had a nice physique, I came to the same conclusion as always. There was no comparison. No one could hold a candle to Alex. As I walked down the hall, I stopped at the connecting door and before I could stop myself I pushed it open a little further.

I felt dirty from the afternoon of being manhandled and slobbered over so I decided on a long hot bubble bath which just reminded me of Alex and got the tears flowing all over again. I realized Alex must have gone to Mississippi for the holiday. I couldn't decide which was worse, constantly hearing familiar sounds from the other side of the house or hearing none at all. I caught myself thinking that I couldn't believe Alex hadn't left a note or said goodbye. But then that was my doing, wasn't it?

And that necklace. I bathed in it because I couldn't bear to take it off. How can you love something so much that represents the greatest pain you've ever felt? After my bath I found myself wandering around the house trying to think of something I could give Alex. I drew a blank and plopped down on the couch depressed and out of sorts. Then my eyes trailed up to the painting over the mantel. The one with the fairy in the swing, trying to let herself go, trying to be free but afraid of the dark clouds looming up behind her. I took it off its nail, carried it down the hall and propped it against the wall on the other side of the door. I stood there a minute and then gave the door another nudge. The more I thought about Alex the more nudges the door got.

Alex came home a few days later. By that time the door was more than three-quarters open. I kept finding reasons to have to go back and forth from bedroom to living room, kitchen to bathroom hoping we'd both pass the door at the same time. Who was I fooling? I made myself stop.

I worried myself sick about how the painting had been received. I could see that it was gone from the hall but that's all I knew. It was about ten o'clock New Year's Eve when I heard brief hammering coming from Alex's bedroom. I rushed to mine and listened and could visualize exactly where it was being hung. Over the dresser directly across from the bed. My hand went to my necklace and I wondered why we were torturing ourselves. Or rather why *I* was torturing *us*.

I went back to the living room and settled down to ring in the New Year with Dick Clark. When I would mute the TV during commercials I could hear the matching audio coming from the other side of the wall. I couldn't help but smile. Alex loved commercials almost more than the shows themselves. Claimed it was Americana at its best. But this is from someone who also loved Johny Quest and never missed a rerun of the old Andy Griffith show.

I managed to hang in there until the ball dropped in Times Square. When Auld Lang Syne began to play I was caught off guard by the welling up of emotion inside me. I couldn't listen all the way through so I cut off the TV, turned out the lights and started down the hall. I could still hear the melody coming from Alex's side. I got to the connecting door and almost walked through it but instead I backed up and slid down the wall across from it and just sat there.

About twenty minutes later I heard the other TV turn off and foot-steps coming down the hall. Alex stopped at the door, too, looked through it and saw me sitting there. I struggled to my feet and stepped up to the threshold. We stood there facing each other like fun house mirror images.

My voice cracked. "You said you'd still be here."

"Well, here I am."

There was a long pause while we waited to see who would make the first move. Alex took a deep breath and let it out, "You stepped out of my life. You're going to have to step back in it."

I tentatively reached out and pushed the door the rest of the way open. I held my breath and took a big 'Mother May I' step through it. It couldn't have been more than a second but it seemed like an eternity. Then I felt myself being scooped up and swung around.

"Oh Alex," I said as I hung on, feeling those strong arms envelope me. "I'm so sorry. I don't know what I want us to be. I don't know what I *can* be. I just know I don't want to be apart any longer."

Alex set me down. "Does that mean slow down?"

"Yes, it means slow down. But it no longer means stop."

52

"Wow."

"Yeah. Wow."

"Did you really say it like that or does it get better with the telling?"

"No, Sharon, that's what we said. Why? Is there something wrong? Does that mean something?"

"No, no. It's just that the two of you have got this great Bogart/Hepburn thing going."

"Oh."

"God I'm sorry. I'm not being at all therapeutic am I?"

"It's OK, really. You're a good listener. I'd rather be listened to than analyzed anyway."

"It's just that I've had so little time to digest it all. I usually have a week between sessions with clients and can sit with what I learn and think about it. What with marathon nights with Alex and seeing you every day, it's all I can do just to absorb it all. I hope that's not too disappointing for you. Therapy is neither quick nor magical. It's a lot of hard work."

"I think I'm beginning to realize that. I suppose I was hoping for the magic wand approach."

"Sorry. No magic wand here. But basically what I hear you saying so far is that your attraction to, and love for, Alex had a head on collision with the image you'd created in your mind of the person you would spend your life with. And that you found it difficult, if not impossible, to merge the two."

"Why is that, though? Alex is so much better than the image."

"We all learn at a very early age that adults pair off. That's one of the reasons why singleness feels so unacceptable. As children we see couplings in everything. Our day to day lives, our families, on TV, in our fairy tales. We start unconsciously creating our ideal fantasy life partner from the start. But all we have to base our choices on is what we see in our everyday lives. It's hard enough as adults to makes decisions that go against what we've been taught, but as children it's virtually impossible. Some of the image is grounded in fairy tales and fantasy but most of it is based on what we're taught is acceptable to our family, our church, our community."

"Let me see if I get this, Sharon. So if as an adult we choose otherwise, the fear we feel is not a fear of the person we've chosen but a fear of losing or being rejected by the groups that helped us form the original image in the first place?"

"Exactly!"

"Oh my God, that makes perfect sense!"

"And, Marissa, if the groups that molded you as a child cannot adjust to your independent choices as an adult then you are eventually forced to make another much more difficult choice. That's where the true strength of character comes in."

"So you do think I'm weak."

"No. I think you're struggling with one of the hardest choices anyone can ever face."

"You're right. Every time I've ever run from Alex is when those two worlds have clashed."

"You can't run the rest of your life, Marissa. That's a miserable way to live."

"Yes, it is. And I don't want to do it anymore."

"So, will I see you tomorrow?"

"If I'm going to stop running I may as well stop now. I'll be here."

"Good. I'll see you then."

Alex

Part Three

53

Wednesday June 9, 1999 9:00 PM

"Okay, no chit chat. Marissa's fine. Sends her love. Start talking."

"You know, Sharon, I'm going to have to report you to the APA."

"Very funny. But right now I'm too exhausted to uphold appropriate boundaries. Once I get the whole story I promise to dazzle you both with my brilliance."

"Or baffle us with your bullshit. Isn't that how that saying goes?"

"Talk, Alex. Talk!"

"Well, where'd we leave off?"

"You and I left off right before Thanksgiving but I know all about that and Christmas and New Year's Eve from Marissa."

"So you don't want to hear my version, huh?"

"Cut it out, Alex. Pouting doesn't work for you."

"So what you're saying is 'move along'. Okay, okay, I'll try and summarize."

"You've got to, Alex. I'm so exhausted I've only got a couple of hours left in me tonight."

"But remember, they're letting me out of here tomorrow and I *know* I can't get you from where we are to present day in a couple of hours. So don't expect miracles?"

"Is that your way of saying you're willing to continue this process after you're discharged?"

"We'll have to. There's no way you could possibly grasp what got me in here if you don't know the whole story."

"You're nothing if not complicated, Alex. So, get a move on."

54

Let's see. She walked out of my life. But since my self-esteem is so high and I know I'm so wonderful I knew she'd be back. So I confidently and happily went about my business and waited for her. Gee, you don't look like you buy that.

Okay, what about this? She walked out of my life. I said to hell with her, who needs her anyway. I went out every night, carousing the bars, entertaining myself in the beds of many beautiful women. No?

How about this? I felt as if all my skin had been peeled away, leaving all my nerves exposed and raw. Every thought of her hurt, every sound from her side was like sandpaper on my body. Even the slightest movement of air around me was painful because it reminded me that the world still marched on and that I might have to live in it without her.

The only thing I could cling to was the way her eyes had said 'I love you' when she said goodbye. I lay in bed every night looking at those damn stars and prayed that whatever I'd seen at that moment would somehow win out. I knew it was out of my hands.

Oh, sure, I fantasized on a daily basis of luring her back, winning her back, storming through that door and whisking her into my arms like in 'An Officer and a Gentleman'. But it wasn't meant to be that way. It couldn't be that way. This was her stuff and she was going to have to come to terms with it.

That's why the painting she gave me for Christmas was so perfect. It was her first reaching out. Her first communication that she was thinking about and realizing what some of her fears were. That and the door creeping open slowly but surely was all that gave me any thread of hope. And let me tell you, I hung on to it for dear life.

When I saw her sitting there on the other side of that door on New Year's Eve my heart crawled up in my throat. It took all the self-control I could muster not to kick it the rest of the way open and go to her. She looked like a lost child in that dark hallway, waiting to be rescued. But my rescuing days were over.

When she stood up and finally stepped through the door I threw my arms around her and whirled her around. I assumed our life together was starting at that moment. And actually it was but not in the way I hoped. She quickly made it clear that we were picking up where we had left off. Back in the midst of uncertainty, hesitation and confusion. But at least she was back.

We sat up that night and talked for a long time. We kept our distance, openly acknowledging that our physical attraction was an issue that really muddied the waters at this point. We talked about our attraction to each other and I understood when she said that making love was something she couldn't do unless she was sure about everything else. She was honest in saying she didn't know when that would be or *if* it would be. She told me about her realization that her pulling away, in the end, had nothing to do with pressure from outside sources. They were convenient justifications that kept her from looking at her own fears.

That made my heart sink because I knew only too well that internal fears were much more difficult to overcome than external threats. My fear of rejection had already been honed to a sharp edge over the previous month and a half. I participated and withdrew like a yo-yo throughout the conversation. One of the aspects of our relationship that had returned immediately was our comfort in confronting each other. As often as I pointed out her circular thinking about things that night, she also didn't hesitate to bring my abandonment reactions to my attention.

When we both felt we had some understanding of where we were, we called it a night. I walked her to the door and we awkwardly gave each other a brief A-frame hug, no full body contact, but even that gave me a zing. We both chuckled at ourselves and said goodnight.

Marissa turned as she walked through the door and gave me a parting shot. She's very good at that in case you haven't noticed.

"Alex, you know, I've given this a lot of thought. If I'm committing to tackling my biggest fears in all of this, then I think you should do the same. You need to find your birthparents." And down the hall she went.

I crawled in bed that night mulling it over. I decided to at least begin to commence to start to consider doing just that. Hey, it was a step.

Even though there was this cloud of indecision hanging over our heads, things were fairly normal for the next few months. I suppose that depends on your definition of normal, though, doesn't it? We tried to just relax and be together. We weren't as inseparable as we had been before, which was probably a good thing. We both needed our down time to think. Marissa continued to go to her parents' house regularly even though her father was by that time ambulatory and making great progress. I wasn't sure if she just needed the time away or if she wasn't ready for Tony to know we were trying to work things out. Either way was all right with me; she didn't need any added pressure.

I don't want you to get the impression that this was a depressing or sad time. It wasn't. We laughed and talked and cooked; watched old movies, argued politics and planned a spring garden. It was pretty much the same as before. We steadily got to know each other better and better. It was actually really nice. Frustrating at times, but then all couples should have to live together for a year without physical contact. It's a great way to find out if you're really made for each other or just horny.

Well, it's true! We only seemed to fuss and fight when the hormones kicked in. That's not what we'd fight about, it was usually little nit picky things, but then we'd retreat to our separate sides and get a grip and everything would be fine for a while longer.

She kept on me relentlessly about the birthparent thing. God, it would make my stomach lurch just to think about it. She made a good point that it would answer all my questions of what really happened once and for all. I didn't know if I wanted my worst fears confirmed. I know, I know. You told me to do it seven years before that. I hope it doesn't hurt your feelings that I listened to her and not you. I wasn't ready back then.

I finally gave in out of the completely wrong motivation. I wanted to show her that I was willing to face my fear and bring it to closure, secretly hoping that might spur her to do the same. We did some research on how to go about it. In the process I considered buying stock in antacids, since I was drinking it by the bottle.

We decided the best place to start was New Orleans. That's where the orphanage was or had been and we could also start digging through old papers, and records of vital statistics. I figured we'd make it less painful by taking a long weekend and I could show her the city. If you recall, I spent a lot of time roaming those streets during grad school in Hattiesburg.

We flew down a few days before the St. Paddy's Day weekend. New Orleans is always festive but really blows it out on this weekend. It would be a great distraction after a couple of days of searching for information, but it wouldn't be as insane as Mardi Gras. I've always been of the opinion that no one should go to New Orleans for the first time during Mardi Gras. Not only can you not appreciate the city but you're liable to get trampled to death.

I had gotten us a room with a balcony in the French Quarter at the Royal Sonesta hotel so Marissa could get the full effect. The temptation to skip our original purpose was strong but she kept prodding me on. I won't bore you with the blow by blow details but as it turned out it was going to be a harder task than we thought.

The orphanage had burned to the ground in 1978. No one seemed to know if any records had been saved. It was never rebuilt and Catholic

Charities had assumed oversight of all adoptions in that area from that point on. We wandered from agency to agency, spending a lot of time sitting in waiting rooms only to find that no one could help us. In all fairness we weren't even sure we were in the right part of Louisiana. One social worker did tell us about a national group that assisted adoptees in their searches. She gave us their Internet address. That was about it for day one. We went back to the hotel and I ordered room service for dinner. We were both exhausted from the flight, the long day and my emotional tension.

Marissa showered and then waited on dinner while I jumped in the shower. I was drying my hair when I heard her practically scream my name. That's how I knew dinner had arrived. I had intentionally ordered standard New Orleans fare knowing that it would freak her out. I came out of the bathroom to see her staring at the trays of food on the dresser. She'd already opened one of the beers and was turning it up when she saw me.

"What the hell is *that*!?" she said, pointing to two of the dishes.

"That would be blackened frog legs there. And barbecued crawfish, heads on, there," I said pointing them out.

"I can't eat that," she moaned.

"Yes you can. But in case you don't like it I got you red beans and rice with andouille sausage, too."

"Oh god, you southerners are so weird."

"This isn't southern. *This* is Cajun. And you're gonna love it." I took the trays to one of the beds and started peeling crawfish for her. "I promise I won't make you suck the heads your first time."

I thought she was going to faint. But after much cajoling and pleading she tried everything and loved it all. That gave me hope that someday I might be able to convince her to move south with me. I'd had about enough of Chicago and snow and brothers that acted like assholes. Even then I couldn't conceive of our not spending the rest of our life together. I always had to watch what I said and how I said it or I would find myself talking about our distant future when she still wasn't a hundred percent sure about our present.

The next day went about the same as the first. Everyone we talked to was very nice and as helpful as they could be. Which wasn't much. We changed our approach somewhat by mid day and spent the afternoon scouring microfilmed newspapers from the month of and the month after my birthdate but no one seemed to have slipped up and printed an announcement that matched the date and time and weight. Those were the only facts I had to go on. That at least let us know, within a reasonable doubt, that the decision to give me up had been made in advance. The last stop was the office of vital records where I got a copy of my birth certificate that was issued to my Mom and Dad immediately upon my adoption. We thought perhaps there might be something there that we could cross-reference.

By then I had managed to divorce myself emotionally and had started getting into it like I was Sam Spade, junior detective. Finally in the late afternoon Marissa tugged at my arm and convinced me to call it quits.

We went back to the hotel and laid all the pieces of information out on the bed and tried to see any possible connection. There wasn't one as far as we could see. But at least we'd gotten the name of the national group. We'd see where that led when we got home.

We decided to stay in that night, too, and rest up for the weekend. We ordered a movie and went to sleep early. I worked hard to let the search go so we could enjoy ourselves the next two days.

55

That Saturday we became tourists. We went to Brennan's for breakfast and walked all over the Quarter. Marissa loved it. We went in and out of what seemed like a hundred shops and spent an hour or more walking around the booths at the open air French Market. We ate muffelettas on the street and had hurricanes at Pat O'Briens. We didn't bother with the Riverwalk Mall although I assured her it was incredible. We went in the old Jax Brewery, walked along the Mississippi River and took a quick tour of the new Aquarium where she had to literally drag me away from the penguin exhibit.

Late that afternoon I got us a good position along the main street that the St. Paddy's parade would come down. While she held our place I ran to a street vendor and got daiquiris. She was like a little kid when the parade floats started coming by. I lost track of her several times as she ran out to vie for the beads and trinkets that were being thrown to the crowd, but she always found her way back.

The sky was starting to darken with ominous clouds and we decided we didn't want to get caught in the rush. We walked up Decatur and turned left on St. Philip to get away from the crowd of the parade. A flash of lightning followed by a crash of thunder obliterated any sounds of nearby people. Two seconds later the bottom dropped out of the sky. Tourists and natives alike began to scurry past, headed for shelter in the bars and shops on Bourbon Street.

I grabbed Marissa's hand and prepared to join the mad dash but her arm tightened and she shook her head.

"I don't mind it and I'm tired of the crowds for now." She smiled and turned her face upwards and let the downpour wash over her.

I loosened my grip on her hand, intending to let go, but she slowly entwined her fingers around mine and kept walking. I coughed several times in an effort to get my heart to start beating again but she seemed oblivious to the coronary she was causing. At the corner of Burgundy, she turned right and headed us toward the old courtyard homes that surround the French Quarter. I followed along, dumbfounded; hoping the rain was adequately disguising my sweating palm.

It was raining like it can only rain in New Orleans. In blinding sheets with steam rising in great clouds from the hot pavement. Not that it doesn't rain in similar fashion elsewhere but New Orleans does it with such elegance and fury all at the same time. I was busy worrying that a bolt of lightning would run down the wrought iron railing from a balcony above and fry us like two unsuspecting pieces of country ham. Marissa, though, seemed to be fueled by the intensity of the storm.

We walked past a deeply recessed alcove which served as the back entrance to one of the old homes. Marissa stopped suddenly, retraced our steps and pulled me in with her out of the rain.

"Well thank God. What's gotten into you? We're going to be so sick tomorrow we'll never get anything accomplished."

"Oh Alex, you can be such a hypochondriac sometimes. Besides, who cares if we do get sick? I've never done anything like this and I'm having a wonderful time. This may be the most fun I've ever had in a single day in my entire life!"

She giggled, threw her head back and shook rainwater all over me. Brain tumor, I thought. Nothing short of a brain tumor could cause such a drastic personality change. She'd been so reserved and cautious over the past few months.

"Marissa, are you all right? Unless I'm losing my mind, I think you just giggled. New Orleans does this to people, you know."

Her excitement and intensity were infectious and I teasingly put the back of my hand to her forehead to check for an imaginary fever. I swear I'll never forget what happened next for as long as I live. She reached up and brought my hand down from her forehead to her cheek and then turned and kissed the inside of my palm.

With her other hand she smoothed the hair from my face, paused, then traced a slightly trembling index finger down and across the drenched shirt clinging to my chest.

Her eyes never left mine, "You don't get it do you? You've never seen me like this because I've never felt like this before. Not and allowed myself to *keep* feeling it for any length of time. I always shut it down as soon as it starts. I'm always amazed that it's even possible to feel like this. I feel so *alive* with you…so in…so…in…uh…"

Poor thing, she got that 'deer in headlights' look that I'd been seeing more and more of lately. I knew what she was going to say and she knew that I knew. I wanted so badly to pressure her into saying it. But if there was one thing I knew, it was that Marissa had to come to me. Completely. And of her own accord.

"…fused. Infused and…uh…invigorated."

Even though she balked and couldn't say it I didn't feel too let down. At least I knew for sure she still felt it. Felt the pull. Felt the connection. The electricity. She dropped her head and stared at her feet like an embarrassed little girl. Her hand was still on my chest but it had gone from seductive fingertip to full palm as if she were bracing herself on me.

I guess I must have looked more disappointed or hurt than I thought I did. She looked up at me, patted my chest once or twice like she was trying to either comfort me or make up her mind about something.

"I'm sorry Alex. I know I've been acting like a crazy woman lately but I've been so scared and so confused. I still am. But it's not doing either one of us any good for me to keep denying the obvious." Heavy sigh here. "You and I both know I have feelings for you that go way beyond friendship."

It wasn't 'I Love You' shouted from the rooftops but to my ears it was close. I reached down with both hands and lifted Marissa's trembling hand from my chest, brought it up to my lips and slowly kissed the back of each finger. She didn't jerk her hand away but she didn't swoon and fall into my arms either. She did, however, back up against the wall and stammer "Oh, God, Alex, I don't know if I'm ready for this".

I gave her hand a squeeze. "I know. That's why I was going to suggest that we go back to the hotel, dry off, order up some hot tea and talk. Just talk."

One of the most intriguing aspects of Marissa is that she is so unpredictable. She let out a sigh of relief that ended with an exasperated snort and harumph kind of thing as we stepped from the shadows into the reemerging late afternoon sunlight.

"What was that for?"

"This, right here, is the major part of the problem."

" Marissa, when you take tangential leaps like that I really wish you'd take me with you."

She turned to face me again. "Don't you get it Alex? Are you that oblivious to the major obstacle here?" She was beginning to slip into the dramatic arm waving and gesturing of her Italian heritage.

"You know, I love it when you do that."

"You're not listening to me. This is important. Had I said what I said back there to any of the men I've known before, and probably most I don't know, I would still be there with a tongue thrust halfway down my throat and a hand groping around inside my blouse. But not you. You kiss my hand and suggest we have tea and talk about it. Don't you understand how weird that is? Refreshing, charming and endearing. But also very weird."

"And this is a problem?"

"Yes it's a problem. The reasons I'm falling in love with you are the very reasons I don't want to. I don't know how to be around you in 'that' way. How to act. Give me a big dumb, one thing on his mind man and I can...well...manipulate him any way I like. But you, you're so...so...'unmanly', I don't know what to do with you!"

She threw her arms up and began walking towards the hotel. I let her go. I must not have been totally hopeless. At least I still liked to ogle her from behind when she walked.

56

It took awhile to stop by the bar, order drinks and carry the tray up to the room myself. I opted for hot chocolate with a very heavy dose of Baileys Irish Cream instead of the tea. 'See there', I told myself, 'I'm not as sensitive as she thinks after all'. If we were really going to confront all this I figured something stronger than chamomile tea was in order. I also brought along a Coke for Marissa just in case. She'd never quite been able to adjust to my Southern habit of hot drinks in warm weather. The closer I got to the room the more I began to rethink my beverage of choice. A bottle of Scotch or a few shots of Tequila would have better prepared me.

I walked in the room and was greeted by a billowing cloud of steam pouring from the half-open bathroom door. 'Here we go with the half open door thing again', I thought. Or was it half closed? It wasn't completely open, which I would have taken as a definite invitation. But then again it wasn't totally closed, which would have been an obvious rejection. And it all would have been a moot point if I had stood there analyzing it much longer. I remembered my roommate my freshman year in college always taunting me, 'For crying out loud Alex, don't just do something, stand there!' So I put down the tray, picked up Marissa's mug and eased through the bathroom door.

The steam swirled in various layers of density around my head. I put the mug on the vanity. Tiny rivers of condensation trickled down the mirror and pooled on the lip of the countertop. I watched several cycles of this phenomenon. My few toiletries were neatly accumulated in a small corner while Marissa's were scattered hither and yon over every remaining square inch. I fought the urge to put everything in some kind of order.

Finding nothing else with which to distract myself in the tiny room, I let my eyes trail to the translucent doors of the shower stall. Marissa had long since finished the ablutions of showering and was now perched on the shallow marble shelf at the back of the enclosure. Her arms braced at her side, feet stretched towards the drain, back arched and head against the tile wall, she seemed unaware of my presence, content to let the water beat a steady cadence down her body.

I was, and still am, certain that I have never seen anyone or anything more sensual, more alluring, more innocently inviting. All I wanted to do was simply sit propped against the far wall and stare for as long as time allowed. Not being a complete fool though, I stepped out of one loosely tied boat shoe and then the other. I started to tug the rain soaked T-shirt out of my shorts when I realized I *was* a fool after all.

I stole one last glance, picked up my shoes and quietly slipped back out the door. You know, everyone says chivalry is dead. No damn wonder. It really sucks.

So I tossed my shoes under the nightstand and let myself out the French doors and onto the wrought iron balcony. I mean, what's New Orleans without a wrought iron balcony to stride out on in your time of deepest, darkest need? I should have been brooding and gazing out over the "big muddy" except I couldn't see it from Bourbon Street so I guesstimated where the river was and brooded in its general direction. I don't know how long I stood there but I was deeply entrenched in this film noir metaphor when a gentle hand on my shoulder brought me back.

"Hey, you OK?"

"Yeah, I'm fine." I couldn't look at her so I kept staring out over the darkening rooftops. "You finally run out all the hot water?"

"No. If you must know, I finally got a crick in my neck waiting for you to make up your mind."

"You knew I was there?"

"Yes."

"Why didn't you say something?"

"Like what, Alex?"

"Oh, nothing elaborate. 'Come here' would have sufficed, I think."

"A naked woman striking a seductive and might I add very uncomfortable pose in a steamy shower doesn't say come here to you? What do I have to do? Hit you over the head?"

"Probably wouldn't hurt," I said and with that she reached up and bopped me hard on the forehead with the heel of her hand.

"*OW!*"

"And don't you dare say 'I could have had a V-8'."

"Well then, what the hell should I say? 'Wow, I could have had you'?"

It was one of those times where your mouth is saying one thing and inside your head is a voice saying 'shut up, shut up, shut up you moron'. She looked at me with those deep brown eyes. Her right eyebrow arched ever so slightly and the set of her mouth took on just a hint of bemusement. The combination had that distinctly 'I'll show you' quality that I've seen her get in the courtroom when her opposing witnesses get sarcastic with her.

I didn't know what to expect although I think in my gut I was catastrophizing that she would turn on her heel and walk out of my life, again. I was about to fall all over myself apologizing and trying to explain that I wasn't rejecting her, that it was because I did love her that I couldn't push anything on her, when she reached down and took my hand and pulled me behind her, back into the room. She left me standing by the nearest bed and went back to close the French doors. When she turned around to face me, she leaned back against the doors and tugged on the end of one of the ties to her robe. My breath caught in my throat as it fell open.

In this incredibly sultry voice she said, "Alex, you've had me for quite awhile now, don't you know that?" And I swear this happened before the line in that Jerry McGuire film.

She pushed herself off the doors and started walking towards me. Her hotel robe was too long for her and dragged the carpet, pulling it further away from her body with each step until it hung on her more like a cape, exposing all but her shoulders.

We may have shared a house for a little over a year and it wasn't like I'd never seen her before. I'm the modest one. There for a while Marissa hadn't given much thought to parading around in her underwear. That was one of the huge changes after New Year's. Funny how when we begin to feel sexual towards someone we get more self conscious around them instead of less.

It seemed to take forever for her to move the few feet to where I was standing. And then she was so close I could smell the soap on her skin and see the pinkish glow across her breasts where the hot water had beaten down on her only a short time ago.

She reached up and ran a hand through my hair and her voice cracked when she said, "I want you to make love to me, Alex."

I've always thought of myself as sexually self-assured. But when she said that, this woman that I'd been in love with, agonized over my desire for for so long, quite possibly since that first night in the elevator, when she said those words all I could think was 'dear God, don't let me pass out'.

You laugh but I'm serious. My head spun. My knees felt like they'd turned to jelly. My heart was pounding in my temples. And I think a tear may have even rolled down my cheek.

I reached down and cupped her chin in my hand and turned her face up to mine. Her eyes were as big as saucers, with a combination of desire and fear, I think. And it was hard to tell which one was winning out at that particular moment. As I bent to kiss her for the first time, right before our lips touched, as if she couldn't feel it radiating from every pore of my body I murmured 'I love you, Marissa'. My lips brushed hers as I said it and I could feel hers part as she let out a moan or a whimper one. It was hard to tell which but the meaning was definitely clear.

For a few moments that's all it was, our lips pressed together. With one hand still on her cheek, I let the other drop to her waist and pulled her against me. It's funny, once I know beyond a shadow of a doubt that I'm wanted and desired then I have no problem taking complete control of the situation. She broke the kiss and jumped back as if startled and I remember thinking, 'Oh God, she's changed her mind'. But she just smiled, kind of embarrassed and said something about my clothes still being damp.

She reached out and started untucking my shirt and I reached down and grabbed the bottom of it to pull it over my head. Just as I had my arms raised all the way over my head I felt her fingertips brush lightly across my chest. By the time I had gotten my shirt all the way off, she was unbuttoning my shorts.

Before I knew it I was stepping out of the last of my clothes. I reached out with both hands and slid the robe from her shoulders and she let it fall to the floor behind her.

You would think that all the sexual and emotional tension that had been building over the past year would have exploded in a torrent of wild, hungry, animalistic sex. But it didn't happen that way at all. Instead, it was the most graceful, flowing, erotically sensual experience you could imagine. There were none of the first time jitters. No awkwardness, no embarrassment. No fumbling, stumbling, oops, pardon me, wait my arm's asleep, ow you're on my hair kind of things. None of that.

When her robe hit the floor it was like the last wall separating us had come tumbling down. It was a silent crash that catapulted us to a whole new plane of existence. Don't roll your eyes at me, Sharon. If you think that sounds hokey, just wait, it gets even better. Time became meaningless. I could no longer feel the physical confines of my body yet I could feel everything. We were standing so close that if we'd been the same height our nipples would have touched. I was certain I could feel the change in the air around me when she inhaled and exhaled.

At the exact same time we both raised a hand. My right and her left. And we touched each fingertip one at a time until our hands were steepled. It had the feeling of a familiar yet long forgotten ritual. I think I had a mind orgasm. Or maybe it was my soul. I don't know.

We both stood there, totally unselfconscious, and watched our hands make love like they had a mind of their own. It was like knowing a symphony so well that you have no need for the sheet music. I held her hand in mine and made slow circles in her palm with my thumb. I moved up each finger one at a time exploring, caressing every inch. Our fingers intertwined and then she began to do same. It felt incredible and it was beautiful to watch, like some kind of intricate hand ballet.

She kept looking from our hands to my eyes and back again with this incredulous look on her face. I don't know if she couldn't believe we were doing what we were doing or if she couldn't believe how tender yet intense it all was. Either way, I could tell she felt that this was like nothing she'd ever experienced before and we hadn't even made it to the bed yet. She started to sway noticeably so I wrapped my arms around her, lifted her up and laid her down on the bed.

She looked up at me with an almost apologetic look in her eyes and started to say, "Alex, I've never…I mean, I don't know…", but I shushed her with a long kiss. Our tongues explored each other for the longest time. Our hands roamed each other's bodies. I felt something wet on my cheek and broke the kiss. There were tears in her eyes but all she said was, "Don't stop."

I kissed the tears away. Kissed her cheeks. Her forehead. The bridge of her nose. And back to her mouth. I buried my face in her hair and drank in the smell of sweet shampoo. I lingered nibbling her neck and collarbone and snuffled her ear like a puppy, which made her squirm and giggle. I kissed her again then rolled her onto her stomach. I straddled her back and she tensed up until I moved her hair aside and began massaging her shoulders. I don't know how long I spent massaging and kissing my way down the length of her back to that little hollow at the base of her spine. I rolled her back over. As I kissed my way around to her stomach, I slid my body up hers until I was facing her balanced on my outstretched arms. She wrapped her arms around my neck and pulled me down on top of her. For the first time the full length of our bodies were pressed against each other. She slipped a leg across the back of my legs and rocked her hips against my thigh. I kissed my way down her neck to her breasts and sucked them like a hungry child. As I slowly kissed my way down the length of her body she surprised me by arching her hips and gently but insistently urging me downward until my tongue slid between her legs. I stroked and teased her with my tongue until she came and then slid first one, then two fingers inside her. She went rigidly still, tightened down on my fingers with her muscles and dug her nails into my shoulders. I was afraid I had somehow hurt her. I looked up at her and she half whispered half gasped that it was okay she just needed to relax. I laid my head on her stomach and she stroked my hair. After a few minutes her muscles relaxed from around my fingers and she began to move against them. Slowly and timidly at first. Eventually with complete abandon. I made love to her like that in every conceivable position, and some that challenged the imagination, for what I later realized must have been hours. I couldn't tell where one orgasm stopped and another started. Her hands never stopped moving over me urging me to keep going. When we were face to face I kissed her hungrily. When we weren't, I kissed whatever I could reach. I would slow down every so often and she'd beg me not to stop until she finally collapsed in my arms.

She burrowed into my chest and I rocked her like a baby. I thought she was still gasping for breath. I know I was. But the movement of her body was too jerky for that. Then I realized she was sobbing. I had never in my life made a woman feel so good and cry so much all in the same night.

"Marissa. Sweetheart," I kept rocking her and stroking her hair. I knew the sweetheart part was a big risk but it just came out. "What's the matter? You can talk to me." But she just shook her head against my chest and cried harder.

57

The sobs had trailed off awhile ago but she still clung to me tightly. I felt her head move.

"Alex?"

"Mmmmmhmmmm."

"Do you love me Alex?"

"Yes. Yes, I do." I kissed the top of her head. She was quiet for a while.

"I mean really, *really* love me."

"To the depth, breadth and height my soul can reach." She laid there a little longer. Then took a deep breath.

"My uncle raped me. Often. Every summer. From the time I was thirteen until I went to college. He's dead now." I hugged her to me tighter.

"That takes away my first option," I said. "I guess all I'm left with is hating him."

"Changes things though, doesn't it?"

"Between us?"

"Yes."

"'No."

She put her head back on my chest and wrapped her arms around me. Squeezed hard enough to break a rib.

"Is that what made you cry?" I asked. She shook her head no. I waited.

"I'm thirty-six years old, Alex. Thirty-six. I've dated a lot of guys. *A lot*. I even thought I loved a few of them but when you break it off as fast as I do they tend to add up over the years."

I chose my response carefully. "Marissa, it's okay. I understand. Incest often results in the, uh…well, the victim being promiscuous. So to speak." In my head I'm thinking, 'how many guys are we talking about here?' So I'm human. I get jealous.

"Don't get all therapy-ish on me Alex. That's not what I'm trying to tell you."

"Sorry. So what are you trying to tell me?"

"I'm trying to tell you that in all those years, with all those guys, I never could…I never would…we didn't ever…". She started to cry again. Broken, tearless gasps. "I never trusted…anyone enough…to let them…make love to me until you…tonight."

There wasn't much I could say to that so I just rocked her and cried with her until she fell asleep.

It must have been the wee hours of the next morning. I was sure I was dreaming. Those very real dreams you have when you hover between sleep and semi-consciousness. I was feeling a tongue circling my nipple. It felt so good that I willed myself not to wake up because if you do you never can get back to quite the same place in the dream. I did try to move though, so I could snuggle down and enjoy this one. But something was keeping me from rolling over. I tried not to focus on it but after a couple of tries I gave up and opened just one eye hoping to not completely wake up.

There was this woman propped up on one elbow leaning over me. Her long dark hair was cascading across my chest and I could feel it caress me as she moved. I couldn't see her face but then I never can when I'm dreaming, but I could see her tongue moving in slow circles over me. I could tell this was going to be a really good one so I closed my eye, if it was ever really open, and put my hand on the back of this woman's head and pulled her into me as a sign of encouragement. I could feel her lips move into a smile and she murmured, "Good morning", and resumed her attentions. I laid there a moment thinking, 'Did I hear that with my ears or was it inside my head where it's supposed to be?' I was still pondering this when suddenly something bit my nipple. Not too hard but enough to get my attention. My eyes popped open as I heard Marissa say, "This is a momentous occasion for me, Alex. If you sleep through it you're going to hurt my feelings."

I thought she would slide up and kiss me but she turned back to my chest. She had not actively brought me to orgasm the night before although I'd certainly not gone unsatisfied. I got the feeling that she was intent on doing just that this morning and she instinctively knew that if we kissed our focus would return to her and a repeat of the night before. After what she had told me about her uncle I knew this would be difficult for her. As significant as the previous night had been in overcoming her fears, being the aggressor now would be even harder for her.

Her movements were stilted and hesitant as if she weren't sure of what she was doing but she didn't stop. I let her go at her own pace even though she was driving me slowly out of my mind. She spent a great deal of time on my chest and stomach. She would kiss her way down and then hit some invisible barrier and start back up. I tried to be lovingly patient. I really did. But finally I took her hand and slid it slowly between my legs and held it there. She tried to pull away but I wouldn't let her. On one hand I knew this could potentially cause her to have a flashback. On the other hand I couldn't wait any longer. She tried to pull away again and said, "Alex, I'm sorry. I can't."

"Yes you can, Marissa. This isn't about the cruelty an old man forced on a young girl. This is about two people, adult people, who love each other and want to share that in every way. If that's not what you want you need to tell me now."

She didn't say anything. I started moving her hand over me showing her how I liked to be stroked. When I felt her pick up the rhythm on her own I let go of her hand and she kept it there. I tried to hold off as long as I could but I'd been waiting for this for over a year. I began to move in time with her and she responded by quickening her strokes. When the first spasms started I pressed her hand against me and held it there until they subsided. I pulled her to me and kissed her hard on the mouth but couldn't hold it because we were both breathing so hard.

She looked at me with this delightfully wicked grin and said, "I did it, Alex. I really did it."

I laughed out loud and said, "Oh God yes, you most definitely did."

She kept grinning that grin and said in that throaty after sex tone that I've come to love, "And I liked it." I felt my eyes roll back in my head. If I'd been standing up I'd have fallen down.

Marissa seemed to think that this was as good a time as any to make up for eighteen years of chastity. I was happy to oblige. We made love from sunrise to late morning. Like silly teenagers. Like wild animals. Like circus contortionists. Like longtime partners. At one point the people in the room next door banged on the wall. We reacted with mortified self consciousness which turned to uncontrollable giggles which led to a playful wrestling match trying to keep each other quiet which led to...well, you can imagine.

At some point during the morning we realized we were starving. It took a twenty-five dollar bribe to get a bellhop to run down to Cafe DuMonde and bring back coffee and beignets. When he came to the room Marissa answered the door wrapped in a sheet from the other bed. She looked like a Greek goddess and smelled like sex. He looked about nineteen and practically drooled on himself. He glanced past her and saw me lying in the bed. He shook his head and stuttered that if during her stay Marissa needed anything at all then he was her man. I called out that if she decided she needed one he'd be the first to know.

Marissa set the coffee on the nightstand, handed me the plate of sugared French doughnuts and told me I was mean. I pulled the sheet off her, blew powdered sugar all over her body and proceeded to lick it off. She decided I wasn't so mean after all.

All the anxiety of the beginning of my birthparent search had faded into the background. I knew it would come back but since I'd made it thirty-one years without them a little bit longer wouldn't make too much difference. We'd gotten about all we would get out of this visit. I knew I was going to have to take this process in baby steps anyway. Just going down there and getting started was more like a toddler's stride. Besides, I had more important things on my mind.

By unspoken consent we stayed in the room all day. We showered and napped. Cuddled and talked. About nothing and everything. But not about our future. That could wait.

58

"So. How was that for moving right along?"

"Jeez, Alex, that may have been more detail than I needed to know."

"I didn't hear you trying to stop me."

"Uh, well...I guess not. I didn't want to throw off your train of thought."

"Yeah, right. Auditory voyeur."

"*Well*...hmmm, this could be a good time to model self awareness and self disclosure for a client. So, yes, I am."

"I thought so."

"You know as well as I do, in our business you almost have to be a voyeur to one extent or another. But I gather consummating the relationship didn't solve all your problems."

"Not hardly, but it was the final step that bound us together. The physical, sexual part of it, while incredible, was actually insignificant compared to the emotional and yes, spiritual experience. The love, the trust, the complete abandon, the commitment. I can't describe it. It *was* our marriage ceremony as far as I was concerned. It was the most precious gift I've ever received and I vowed at that moment to honor, cherish and protect it, forever. Actually it felt more like I was renewing a vow I'd made to her eons before. I know you struggle with this, Sharon, but I'm telling you, this is not Marissa's and my first time around together. Not by a long shot."

"All right, Alex, you're creeping out of my area of expertise here. And if you ever tell anyone I said this I'll vehemently deny it. But I believe you."

"You do?"

"Yes. I do. I don't know where it's coming from exactly, and it goes against all my scientific beliefs and training. But if ever there were soul mates…"

"Yeah, I know. It boggles my mind, too, sometimes."

"I'm about to stray way outside the boundaries of professional ethics and you've probably known this for years, anyway. But if I weren't married to one of the most wonderful men God put on this planet…well, let's just say Marissa's a very lucky woman."

"Well, Sharon, I'm flattered."

"Ha, now *I'm* feeling emotionally narcoleptic. I wonder if it's catching?"

"Go home. Get some sleep. You need to be fresh for my dishonorable discharge tomorrow."

"Oh that's right. Do you think society's ready for that?"

"Screw society. I just hope Marissa's ready."

"Ready and willing I assure you. You've both got some hard work ahead of you but I'm glad you both realize what you've got together. I'll see you tomorrow."

Marissa

Part Three

59

Thursday June 10, 1999 9:00AM

"Good morning, Marissa. Come on in. Ready for the big day?"

"Absolutely. I feel like a cat that's been granted a tenth life."

"That's a good analogy. The two of you have certainly had more than your share of trials and tribulations."

"Isn't that the truth. How's Alex doing? Ready to come home, I hope. I keep worrying that might not be the case. I mean, how much can one person take?"

"Don't start beating yourself up again. Alex may be getting discharged from the hospital, but you're the one who's actually coming home, don't you think?"

"You're right. We've both been emotionally gone but in this case it's my coming back that's enabling Alex to do the same. So how did last night go?"

"Oh, you're not going to believe this, but we got all the way from Thanksgiving through New Orleans in one sitting."

"You're right, I don't believe it."

"I understand the struggle you went through. Tell me how it felt to resolve it. To finally take that next step."

60

I suppose most people these days couldn't begin to fathom how we could know each other for more than a year, practically live together for most of it, and not have a physical relationship. I've heard some say that it took that long for Alex to finally wear me down. I've even heard 'brainwash' a time or two. But I guess you know by now that it wasn't like that at all. Alex never took the initiative to move our friendship to a relationship or our relationship to the bedroom. I think deep down we both knew from the very beginning that we would be together although my conscious mind refused to acknowledge it. When we were in New Orleans everything I'd been feeling for months finally welled up inside me and somehow I found the courage to say it out loud.

And when I told Alex I wanted to make love I remember being so overwhelmed for a moment everything went brown. I'd never said that to anyone, ever. I was afraid I couldn't follow through even though I knew it's what I'd been leading up to, what I'd been wanting for almost a year. But everything was so natural. Like we'd been together for years. As though we'd made love hundreds of times. And then I felt myself being swept up and laid on the bed. I don't know why but it never occurred to me that Alex was strong enough to do that. I'd dated more than my share of men, several of whom were the big, strong burly type, but none of them had ever picked me up much less swept me off my feet and taken me to bed. But then, I never wanted them to. Funny thing is, we could have stopped right there and most of my romantic fantasies would have already been fulfilled.

Staring up into Alex's face at that moment I knew I had never been so loved and cared for in my life. And I realized that I actually wanted to return all those feelings although I wasn't sure I knew how. I'd known for a long time that I loved Alex on an emotional level but except for those late night fantasies in the privacy of my own mind and bed, I never thought I'd be able to take it to the physical level. Partly because of Alex but mostly because of my own issues.

But here I was, not just wanting to please so that someone would continue to want me and care about me. But wanting, craving even, to lay myself wide open and allow someone to walk around at will in that inner part of me that I had so carefully guarded all my life. It was the first time that I understood the difference between having sex and making love. That you could do both at the same time or you could do either one without the other. And that I'd only ever experienced the lesser of the three possibilities.

I realized that I was a thirty-six year old emotional virgin. My hymen had been broken brutally when I was thirteen. My heart had been broken off and on ever since. But this was the first time my defenses had ever been broken. I was on the verge that day of offering up not just my body, but my heart and soul, for safekeeping to another person. And I think I was able to do it because from the moment we touched I had a deep sense that I'd given it all to Alex McKinley many times before and that I would again, over and over, in different times, in different bodies, with different names. I know Alex talks about that concept easily and openly and my heart tells me it's true. But my mind, my intellect, tells me it's crazy. It's impossible. It's wishful, romantic thinking that helps me justify the attraction and the relationship. I suppose that's where the confusion comes in. When I listen to my heart, my body, my emotions, I know that I'm in love beyond my wildest imagination. But every so often my head takes over and I begin to question it all. And I don't know if the questions are legitimate or if I simply feel undeserving of being so happy and so loved. I hate to think I keep sabotaging the best thing I could ever have simply because the intensity of it frightens me. Most people would kill just to experience once what I've got the opportunity to have for a lifetime.

I was glad all these thoughts didn't start while we were in New Orleans. If they had, I probably would have run as fast and as far away as I could. Luckily, there was no way my head had a chance to take over after that experience. We basked in it the whole next day until our plane left. We were so wrapped up in each other we almost forgot to go to the airport.

But the reality of what we were in for set in on the plane. I felt like the previous forty-eight hours was written all over my face. In my mind's eye I started seeing all the people in those groups we talked about yesterday. My family, my church, my friends and co-workers. I started imagining judgment and condemnation in the eyes of total strangers on the plane. I wanted to lay my head on Alex's shoulder but stopped myself several times. We ended up spreading a blanket over us and holding hands beneath it. I could hear my mother going on and on about how disgusting public displays of affection were.

Chicago was a different place than when we'd left four days before. I'd left with a friend and come back with a lover. Back to family, friends, and co-workers who wouldn't accept the choice that I'd made. Who would refuse to even try. I wasn't sure I could handle it.

61

"Do you still feel that way, Marissa? Is that part of what's going on now? I don't have a clear picture of exactly what's troubling the two of you. You keep talking about running away from Alex. Did you run *to* someone this last time? Is that what prompted Alex to go to the reservoir with a gun? In the intake the description of the events from the other day mentions Alex going to a motel and getting the gun out of your car. Were you there with someone else?"

"His name's Eric. And he's the father of my baby. Yes, I was there with him but I was there to tell him it was over. I was telling him I love Alex. You just don't understand. It's more complicated than you can possibly imagine and I just can't get into it right now."

"And why is that?"

"Because they're discharging Alex in about thirty minutes and all I can focus on is getting home and trying to put our life back together!"

"Marissa, calm down. It's going to be all right. We'll go up in just a minute and take care of all that. I just want to know if you realize that the two of you are at a crossroads in your relationship and you may not be able to fix it by yourselves. We haven't spent these last three days together just because it's mandatory. I care a great deal about Alex and I'm growing to like you, too. The two of you are in trouble and I want to help. I may not have demonstrated much more than the ability to listen up to this point but I do have the skills. However, you both have to commit to seeing this through. It's clear to me that there's more to this story than I thought and it needs to be told before we can do anything long-term, therapeutically speaking. I just want to be sure that your avoidance of talking about…was it Eric? That your avoidance is really about lack of time today and not about something else."

"Damn it, Sharon, don't you make me cry right before I see Alex. I'm just scared, that's all. It's one thing to tell the story. It's something else entirely to force yourself to look at your behaviors and fears and motivations. It kills me to know how hurtful I've been. I'm really afraid to look too closely at the reasons why. I want us to spend the rest of our lives together. What if I'm not strong enough?"

"Whoa, slow down. You're jumping way, way ahead. I just want the two of you to commit to a third party helping you through this. It doesn't even have to be me. Talk it over when you get home and let me know."

"Talk it over? First of all, I like you and trust you. Secondly, do you think either one of us could possibly start over telling this story to someone else? No way. As much as it scares me I know I've got to do this and I want to do it with you, if that's all right."

"That's fine. Let's set you up with another appointment and then go check Alex out of this place."

"Thank you, Sharon. Thank you so much for everything."

Epilogue

Thursday June 10, 1999 10:00AM

Nancy McLean, the ward nurse for the sixth floor, breezed into the room with a clipboard braced against her hip and pushing a wheelchair with one hand. "Tara Alexandra McKinley?"

"Yes, Nancy. We've worked together for over a year now. There's no need to be so formal."

"Oh I know, Alex. It's just that no one up here has ever known your full name. I think it's pretty."

"Ugh!"

"Oh come on," Sharon said. "It's not that bad. Although you certainly don't strike me as a Tara."

"My mother was a big Gone With The Wind fan," Alex muttered with a disgusted look.

Sharon guffawed. "Your Mother named you after a house? Oh, that's priceless!"

"I'll have you know it was not a house, it was a plantation! Marissa, get me out of here before I suffer any more indignities."

Trying hard not to laugh, Marissa pushed the wheelchair to where Alex was sitting. "Your chariot awaits oh knight."

"That's what I mean about indignities. I am perfectly capable of walking out of here on my own two feet."

Sharon just shook her head. "Get your hard headed, bullet riddled butt in that wheelchair and let this woman take you home."

Marissa reached down and smoothed the hair from Alex's forehead.

Alex reached up, taking both of Marissa's hands. As their fingers intertwined Alex moved their hands down until they came to rest cupping Marissa's bulging belly.

Alex looked up into Marissa's eyes and nodded, "Yes, home. I'm ready for the three of us to go home."